SPECIAL MESSAGE TO READERS

THE ULVERSCROFT FOUNDATION
(registered UK charity number 264873)

was established in 1972 to provide funds for research, diagnosis and treatment of eye diseases. Examples of major projects funded by the Ulverscroft Foundation are:-

- The Children's Eye Unit at Moorfields Eye Hospital, London
- The Ulverscroft Children's Eye Unit at Great Ormond Street Hospital for Sick Children
- Funding research into eye diseases and treatment at the Department of Ophthalmology, University of Leicester
- The Ulverscroft Vision Research Group, Institute of Child Health
- Twin operating theatres at the Western Ophthalmic Hospital, London
- The Chair of Ophthalmology at the Royal Australian College of Ophthalmologists

You can help further the work of the Foundation by making a donation or leaving a legacy. Every contribution is gratefully received. If you would like to help support the Foundation or require further information, please contact:

THE ULVERSCROFT FOUNDATION
The Green, Bradgate Road, Anstey
Leicester LE7 7FU, England
Tel: (0116) 236 4325

website: www.foundation.ulverscroft.com

INTRIGUE IN ROME

Gail Bennett's working holiday in Rome takes an unexpectedly sinister turn as soon as she arrives at her hotel. Why does the receptionist give out her personal details to someone on the phone? Who is the mysterious man she spies checking her car over? Soon she meets Paul, a handsome Englishman keen to romance her — but he is not what he seems. And how does Donato — Italian, charming — fit into the picture? Gail knows that one of them can save her, while the other could be the death of her . . .

Books by Phyllis Mallett in the Linford Romance Library:

LOVE IN PERIL
THE TURNING POINT
LOVE'S MASQUERADE
POOR LITTLE RICH GIRL
ISLE OF INTRIGUE
HOUSE OF FEAR
DEADLY INHERITANCE
THE HEART IS TORN
SINISTER ISLE OF LOVE
MISTRESS OF SEABROOK
HER SEARCHING HEART
TIDES OF LOVE

PHYLLIS MALLETT

INTRIGUE IN ROME

Complete and Unabridged

LINFORD
Leicester

First published in the United States of
America in 1977

First Linford Edition
published 2016

*A catalogue record for this book is available
from the British Library.*

ISBN 978–1–4448–3057–6

Published by
F. A. Thorpe (Publishing)
Anstey, Leicestershire

Set by Words & Graphics Ltd.
Anstey, Leicestershire
Printed and bound in Great Britain by
T. J. International Ltd., Padstow, Cornwall

This book is printed on acid-free paper

1

I could not suppress the fluttering sense of anticipation that filled me as I drove steadily in the flow of traffic on the outskirts of Rome. But I had waited impatiently for this holiday and, although there would be a measure of work attached to it, I had every intention of enjoying myself to the fullest. It was a bright afternoon in June, and the windows of my white Corsa 1.4 automatic were wide open, admitting a breeze that ruffled my light brown hair. I frowned slightly behind my sunglasses, for despite having made the long trip from England in easy stages, I was tired of driving. It would have been less exhausting had I travelled by air or by boat and train, but this was to be a working holiday and I would need the car, though I had been warned that parking was difficult in the Eternal City.

A reckless blue Ferrari appeared

from nowhere, overtook me, and pulled in front much too close for comfort. I slammed my foot on the brake pedal, uttering a mild imprecation against road hogs of all nationalities. A quick glance in the rear-view mirror frightened me; the vehicle behind was much too close for comfort. But the Ferrari darted forward again and I accelerated into the space he vacated, sighing heavily in exasperation as I watched the Ferrari's erratic progress through the stream of traffic. It was like a preying shark amongst minnows, powering effortlessly in expert hands, darting forward, cutting in sideways, but always overtaking the line of vehicles. Horns sounded belligerently as the more aggressive drivers protested at such inconsiderate road usage, but the Ferrari left us standing, and I took firm control of my emotions and concentrated on motoring carefully over the final stage of the journey that had brought me to my destination.

This was my first visit to Italy. Two years before, I had spent a week in

Switzerland, and last year I'd toured France. But I always combined pleasure with business. As a freelance journalist and short-story writer, I used my annual holiday to gain local colour and facts that would sustain my literary activities during the rest of the year, and so far the system had worked successfully.

I smiled wryly as I recalled my mother's farewell advice. She had been genuinely worried because her only daughter was travelling alone to foreign places, and I was sorry that she could not accompany me — Mother was not well enough to travel.

'Gail, you'll be careful, won't you? One hears of so many dreadful happenings these days,' she had warned me. 'I don't think it's right for a woman to travel alone around Europe.'

'At twenty-four, Mother, I can take care of myself,' I had responded. 'It isn't as if this is the first time I've been abroad alone. It'll be all right, and I'll have my laptop, so I can talk to you on Skype every day.'

That had been our parting, and within an hour of leaving home in Sussex I had forgotten Mother's concern. My father, a successful author of popular fiction, was dead. I had inherited my wanderlust from him, as well as his fluent ability with words — and his gambling instinct. I didn't gamble in the literal sense, but was endowed with a rash streak that, coupled with an overwhelming optimism, induced me to take chances that other people would not contemplate. It was my love of complete freedom and my dislike of convention that had caused me to leave a secure job with the local newspaper in Croxley and attempt to earn my living as a freelance writer. It could make my existence precarious at times, but I had made a fair success of the venture, much to the surprise of my friends and former colleagues.

There was no opportunity to see the sights here yet; I had to watch for road signs. I had booked a room in advance in a three-star hotel in the region of the

Piazza de Spagna, and had made a list of the points of interest I wanted to see in the two weeks I planned to spend in Rome. But work could wait. First, I was going to relax and enjoy myself.

The hotel proved to be small and old, but there was a courtyard for the car. I sighed with relief at having found the place without any trouble, and alighting, stretched thankfully to get the kinks out of my back and neck. My luggage consisted of two heavy cases, my laptop, and an overnight bag. I removed these from the boot, double-checked that the car was locked, and struggled wearily into the lobby.

The receptionist at the desk was an olive-skinned, mature woman who spoke such good English that I didn't get the opportunity to use my Italian.

'Gail Bennett,' I announced, dropping my cases.

'Ah, I have your reservation,' was the friendly reply. 'You have travelled far, no?'

'Yes, and I'm exhausted!' I signed the

register as she selected a key and then picked up one of my cases. We ascended two flights of stairs before reaching my room, which overlooked the courtyard. I went immediately to the bed and sat down with a long sigh of relief, smiling at the receptionist. 'This might be Rome, and I've waited a long time to get here, but right now all I want is a bath and a rest.'

She made a clicking noise with her tongue. Her brown eyes were intense and penetrating. 'There is no bath,' she said, and, smiling at my swiftly changing expression, pointed at a door on the right. 'We modernised last year. We have showers now.'

I nodded, smiling in relief, for I'd had a sudden vision of trying to wash in a small basin or something equally primitive. She departed, wishing me a pleasant stay at the hotel and a happy holiday in Rome. When the door closed behind her I pushed myself wearily off the bed and opened the overnight bag to get my toilet bag, and then left a trail of travel-creased clothes on the floor between the bed and the bathroom door.

It was pure ecstasy to stand under the refreshing jets of hot water that gushed over my tired body; and although I would have preferred a bath in which to lie and soak, I felt my long-suffering muscles gradually relaxing. The shower worked a miracle on my nerves and flesh, and I towelled myself briskly, then slipped into a dressing gown and wrapped a hand towel around my head. I contemplated the comfort of the bed, but a writer's mind is never off duty, even when the laptop is switched off and the top is screwed on the fountain pen. I went to the window, peered out from behind a curtain to take my first look at the Roman skyline, and glanced down to check my car in the courtyard immediately below the window. I drew back slightly when I saw a man standing behind the Corsa. He had a pen and a notebook in his hands and was obviously writing down my car number.

Had I fallen foul of the law? I had studied Italian motoring regulations carefully, for any infringement could result in an instant fine. But the man was not in uniform and did not have the air of a policeman about him. In fact, he was furtive, continually glancing around at the hotel entrance as if afraid that someone might appear and warn him off. He was stocky and middle-aged, in shirt sleeves, and wearing beige trousers. From my angle of view he seemed foreshortened, which gave him a dwarfish appearance, making him seem as wide as he was tall. Then suddenly he looked up swiftly, straight at my window, as if he had felt the power of my gaze or knew that I was in this particular room. His features were coarse and heavy, and there was a small round bald patch on the crown of his curly black hair.

I drew back quickly, frowning. Was he a thief? But I discounted that theory immediately. He wouldn't have written down the number of my car if he was planning to steal it. I remained watching him intently and, when he reached out and tried to open the lid of the boot, I moved away from the window, untying the cord of my dressing gown and letting it slip to the floor. I whipped the towel from my head, and it took me only a few seconds to pull on jeans and a blouse before returning to the window. The man was now trying to open the driver's door — attempting to get into the vehicle in broad daylight! I was astounded by his audacity, and yet I did not think to lean out of the window and shout at him. Some intuitive sense had me turning and running from the room. I meant to confront him, for obviously he was up to no good.

My slippers made no sound on the carpeted stairs during my hurried descent. I reached the lower flight to the entrance hall, engrossed with the inquisitive stranger acting so suspiciously around my car. But the high-pitched voice of the receptionist speaking rapidly in Italian attracted my attention, for she mentioned my name.

I paused to listen, hidden from her view by the corner of the wall to the left of her desk.

'I have been trying to contact you for the past twenty minutes,' she was saying in an urgent tone. 'You wanted to know when the Englishwoman arrived. Well, she is here now. Yes, she's travelling alone. That's right. Her name is Gail Bennett. Her car is a white Corsa with a 2012 number plate. I expect she will be going out this evening for her first look around the city. Is that all you wanted to know? You'd better send someone around before she leaves and I will point her out to him so there can be no mistake. Yes, I'll do that. And don't forget you owe me ten thousand euros for this information.'

The sound of the telephone receiver being replaced jerked me out of the paralysis of shock that seized me as I mentally translated her gabbled words. Something froze into a solid lump in my breast, and I drew a deep breath to get rid of the choking sensation clutching at my throat. What was that all about? And who was the man in the courtyard taking such an interest in my car?

I had temporarily forgotten about the man, but now I was disinclined to confront him, and realised that it might be better not to let the receptionist discover that I had overheard her telephone conversation. Turning quickly to return to my room, I lost my left slipper, and turned in dismay as it went bouncing down the stairs. The receptionist heard the faint sound and came around the desk to the foot of the stairs, her face expressing surprise and concern when she saw me. For a moment guilt stained her dark features, and then she bent, picked up the slipper and held it out to me. I had to descend the stairs to collect it, and she fixed my gaze with hypnotic power as she tried to read my expression.

'Is there something you want?' she asked in Italian.

'I'm sorry, but I don't speak Italian,' I said without hesitation, and wondered what had induced me to lie. But I did not want her to know that I had understood her telephone conversation, for she was obviously using her native tongue now in an attempt to discover if I understood the language.

She changed to English. 'Is something wrong? Are you going out in slippers?'

I smiled disarmingly, carefully avoiding contact with her hand when taking my slipper from her, and I took my time replacing it on my foot. I sat down on the bottom step and looked at my feet for the moment it took to push my toes into the slipper. I was in control of my facial expression, but the chill sensation inside me had shocked my presence of mind. A tiny voice in my subconscious was demanding more information about this perplexing situation, and all I really understood was that I had to pretend to know nothing.

'I left something in my car,' I said, regaining my feet. 'I'm not planning to go out just yet. I need to rest before sightseeing.'

'And you don't speak any Italian?' she persisted, her features taut, her dark eyes filled with a harsh glitter. She was clearly suspicious of me. But her expression of guilt was fading now and she seemed reassured by my ignorance. She smiled, and I wondered at her duplicity and why she was passing on my personal details to some anonymous person who was willing to pay for that information.

'I speak a little French and some German,' I replied, 'but haven't got around to learning Italian yet. It sounds such a delightful language, too; so warm and lively. You speak very good English.'

'I learned it many years ago.' She nodded slowly, and I congratulated myself on turning the conversation so adroitly. 'May I go to your car for you?' she added.

'Thank you, but no.' I smiled in what I hoped was a casual manner, injecting friendliness into my tone. Her suspicion had faded and she seemed satisfied that I had no inkling of what had been said over the telephone. 'I've left my car keys in my room, anyway. I shall have to fetch them.'

A sigh of relief escaped me as I turned and ascended the stairs, aware that she was watching me intently. I moved casually, as if I hadn't a care in the world, but almost collapsed when I was out of her sight. I forced myself upwards, gripping the stair rail, my legs trembling, for my delayed reaction had set in with its weakening effect. If she could have seen me at that moment she would had realised that I'd overheard and understood her phone call.

I entered my room and sank down on the bed, only to spring up and run to the window. But I need not have bothered. The man who had been so interested in my car was gone, and he was nowhere in sight on the small part of the road in view.

The conversation I had overheard was running through my mind like a crazy tape-recording. Someone was interested in my arrival, and the receptionist had been bribed to divulge it. An Englishwoman travelling alone! My mother's voice seemed to insert itself into the shocked turmoil gripping my thoughts. 'One hears of so many dreadful happenings these days, Gail,' she had counselled, and my reply had been that I could take care of myself. But could I? This would not be some ardent young Romeo's attempts to make my acquaintance. Someone had gone out of his way to discover when an unaccompanied woman would arrive at the hotel, and had spent good money to ensure that he got the information.

I felt afraid. My joyous sense of anticipation had been overlaid abruptly by frightening shock. Fear is always more potent when it is rooted in the unknown, and I certainly had no idea what kind of sinister web was enveloping me.

Outside my window lay the Eternal City of Rome, bathed in sunshine and warmth. But there were shadows in obscure corners, and I sensed that somehow I had stumbled into one of those corners where unreality and danger lurked. Perhaps it was my intuition, but I was certain that trouble, possibly danger, awaited me out there in the streets. It was too late now to wish that I had paid heed to Mother's warning.

2

The first flush of shock ebbed away as I sat on the bed contemplating the two incidents. My journalistic mind began asking pertinent questions, and I half-convinced myself that there were logical explanations for what had occurred. The man checking my car could have been a plain-clothes policeman — there was a GB plate on the back of the Corsa and, as far as Italians were concerned, it was a foreign car — or he may have been engaged in the harmless hobby of collecting car numbers. I dismissed him from my mind and turned my thoughts to the telephone conversation I had overheard.

What possible reason could the receptionist have for passing on such information? I had booked in advance, so she would have known something about me before my arrival. The words that I had overheard returned to my mind with frightening clarity. Someone had wanted to know when I arrived, had I come in a car, and was I alone. That someone even knew my name and would get a look at me the moment I left the hotel — had even paid money for the information. Obviously money had induced the receptionist to talk, but who wanted the knowledge, and more importantly, why?

I considered all the more frightening reasons, such as kidnapping for ransom, or being sold into slavery — I didn't know if that particular vice was operating in Italy, and I had no desire to gain first-hand experience. But I was not wealthy enough to be held for ransom, and tried to reassure myself that there had to be a more reasonable explanation.

Perhaps the receptionist passed on details of her foreign guests to an acquaintance who was a travel guide. That was feasible, but my intuition indicated that the telephone conversation had held a sinister note; and the receptionist's nervous manner when she realised I might have overheard what she said had emphasised a serious undercurrent.

I was tired from travelling, and it was possible that my mind was overwrought. Gazing from my window, and careful to remain out of sight of anyone in the street, I considered what course of action to take. I could confront the receptionist, confess that I spoke and understood Italian very well, and demand an explanation from her; or I could contact the police and report what had happened. But I was a foreigner here, and the Italian police might not take my suspicions seriously. And if I confronted the receptionist, I should only succeed in informing her of my knowledge and place myself at an even greater disadvantage.

There could be little danger to me if I stayed in the crowds of tourists flooding the city. The hotel had other guests, and there might be some English tourists with whom I could strike up a friendship. I shrugged off my fears and decided to reserve judgement of the situation. But that sense of unreality gripped my mind, and a dulling pall of anticlimax destroyed the rapturous anticipation that had risen to a pleasant crescendo inside me. As I lay down on the bed, I feared that I had made a negative start to my holiday.

I glanced at my watch. It showed a few minutes to one p.m., and I decided that a good meal would give me fresh heart. I dressed in jeans and a blouse, descended to the ground floor, and experienced an uncharacteristic sense of diffidence upon entering the dining room. I sat at a side table by an inner wall, feeling lonely and pensive, my excitement dampened by what had happened. I ordered an Italian aperitif, the Americano, a mixture of sweet vermouth and bitter Campari; and while I sipped it I studied the menu and my fellow guests.

There were a dozen small tables, now all occupied, and a lot of conversation going on — I recognised French, German, and heard a couple of languages I was not familiar with. The waitress approached.

The piccato appealed to me — veal cutlet fried in butter and sprinkled with herbs and spices — and I ordered it. Since I was in Italy and it was the custom, I asked for a glass of red wine and, when the waitress pointed out that Chianti was too heavy to drink in hot weather, I agreed and settled for Valpolicella. Then I sat back and studied the assembly, trying to guess which of them was watching me with evil intent.

A man appeared in the doorway, and my gaze flickered immediately to his powerful figure. Aware that subconsciously I was expecting the receptionist to point me out to some stranger, I fought down a momentary pang of panic. He glanced around the room, and when he moved in my direction I could not prevent a sudden rush of tension. Sipping the Americano, I turned my head as if I had not seen him; but I was aware of his approach and did not look up until he was beside the table and coughing politely to attract my attention.

When I turned my gaze to him I saw

a confident smile on his handsome face. He was over six feet tall and fair-haired — one of the best-looking men I had ever seen — and his blue eyes were wide and alert under slender brows. He was in his late twenties, I assumed, and he was not Italian. A glance at the breast pocket of his navy blazer confirmed my judgement, for it was adorned with an emblem embroidered in gold thread that indicated he was a member of an English sailing club. I was instantly impressed by his appearance, which doesn't often happen to me.

'Would you mind if I shared your table?' He spoke in English, his deep tone filled with pleasing undercurrents that sent a delightful thrill through me. But with the receptionist's telephone conversation in the forefront of my mind, I was suspicious of him, and my fears must have shown in my expression, for his smile faded as he anticipated a refusal. I glanced around, saw that there were no vacant tables, and forced a smile as I nodded.

'Be my guest.' I moved my chair slightly and sipped my drink nonchalantly, I hoped.

'You're English!' His smile returned as he sat down. He possessed a great deal of natural charm and more than his share of personal magnetism. 'The receptionist mentioned this morning that an Englishwoman was due to arrive today.'

'I got in a couple of hours ago.' There was a cold edge to my tone that I had not intended, and nervousness and suspicion added an abrasive quality to my voice. I set down my glass and made an effort to present my normal self. 'No need to ask if you're English,' I added in a softer tone, glancing once more at the emblem on his blazer.

'Does it show that much?' His smile was engaging, and friendliness was reflected in his gleaming eyes. He was clean-shaven, and wore his blond wavy hair slightly long; curling at the temples and the nape of his neck. Laughter lines showed clearly, indicating a cheerful disposition, and his face was quite tanned. 'I'm Paul Russell,' he introduced himself. 'I have two weeks of my holiday left.' He paused and gazed expectantly at me.

'Gail Bennett,' I responded. 'I'm on a working holiday.' My tone was still sharper than normal, and must have given him the impression that I was standoffish. But his smile did not falter, and he seemed not in the least concerned by my closed manner. His smile was warm and friendly.

'I'm an insurance agent in London,' he volunteered. 'I've wanted to come to Rome for as long as I can remember, and this is my year for it.'

'Are you alone?' My question struck like a knife thrust.

'Yes.' He smiled, somewhat wistfully. 'And it does get pretty lonely sometimes.'

My meal arrived at that moment and the waitress took his order. He asked for fritto misto alla Romana, a mixed grill, and ordered Valpolicella.

'You sound as if you speak very good Italian,' I remarked, and began my meal, for the aroma coming from my plate made me realise just how hungry I was.

He smiled. 'I speak Italian and Spanish, and at the moment I'm picking up German in my spare time. I seem to have a flair for languages. Do you speak Italian?'

My eyelids fluttered as I glanced down at my plate before answering, aware that he was watching me with those penetrating blue eyes. He had such a pleasing appearance that I could not believe he was anything other than genuine.

'No,' I lied, still wondering if he could be the person who had been on the other end of the line when the receptionist gave out my details. 'But I have a phrasebook, which should help. If I can't pronounce the words I can always point out the phrase in the book.'

His laugh was attractive, deep and

steady, and he shook his head slowly. 'You'll probably find the book won't contain the particular phrase you need. But sign language goes a long way, and many Italians do speak English.'

He paused and glanced around the dining room, giving me the opportunity to study his profile. His chin was strong, his lips sensual; his nose straight and finely bridged beneath a rugged forehead. He was the kind of man I usually characterised as the hero in my romantic short stories, and if I hadn't been suspicious of everyone right then I would have entertained an idea of spending some of my holiday in his company. He looked at me, turning his head quickly, almost taking me by surprise, and his blue eyes seemed to bore right through me, as if he could read my innermost thoughts.

'So, you're on a working holiday,' he commented. 'May I ask what it is you do?'

'I'm a freelance journalist and short-story writer. I've come to Rome to get background information for a series of travel articles, which I propose writing toward the end of this year in time for next summer. My holiday will be a mixture of business and pleasure.'

'That's very interesting.' He thanked the waitress when she paused at the table to set down his aperitif. 'I've never met a writer before.'

'I always had a flair for English. My father was a successful fiction writer, and he had a big influence on my early ambitions.'

'Really!' He leaned forward, holding my gaze. 'Perhaps I've read his work.'

'He wrote crime thrillers.' My voice had a catch in it. 'He's dead now.'

'Oh, I'm sorry.' The sparkle left his eyes. 'Are you here alone?'

I tensed, and could not control my face quickly enough to prevent a shadow crossing it. To my suspicious mind that was a leading question. Then I nodded slowly. The receptionist had already passed on that information about me, so I would not betray myself by admitting it. 'Yes, I'm alone — no one to divert me from what I have to do. I live in my own little world most of the time. Not very good company for a companion wanting to enjoy herself.'

'Herself?' he queried, his keen gaze probing my face.

'My mother.' My lips softened as I pictured Mother's face. 'I wanted her to come with me, but she's afraid of travelling. She survived a plane crash — Father didn't. That was five years ago. Father had been on a working holiday, getting local colour for a book.'

'How tragic! Is that why you're using a car?'

'Partly.' I frowned as I considered his question. 'How did you know I came by car?'

'I saw the Corsa in the courtyard when I came in, and it wasn't there when I went out earlier, plus there's a GB plate on the back. You're the only other English tourist here.'

His meal arrived then, and silence settled between us. I watched him intently whenever he was not looking at me, and noted that despite his smooth manner he seemed to be constantly on the alert, darting quick glances around as if afraid someone unpleasant was sneaking up on him. He also shot glances at me, as if hoping to catch me with my guard down. I struggled against my suspicions, afraid they would show in my eyes. When I had finished my meal he was barely halfway through his, and I sighed with relief as I arose.

'It's been nice talking to you,' I said, and he startled me by dropping his knife and reaching out quickly to grasp my wrist. My eyes widened in shock, but he smiled in a most captivating way.

'I'd like to warn you to remember that this isn't England,' he said softly. 'When you're wandering around with your head in the clouds and your imagination working overtime, do try to keep at least one foot on the ground.' He paused, but I remained silent. For the first time since we'd met he seemed to be uncertain of himself, hesitant, his bright blue eyes narrowing slightly. 'Look, half my holiday is over, and I've already taken in most of the sights. If you'd care to have a friendly guide who can speak English and Italian, I'd be more than happy to accompany you. It would be an experience for me to discover how a writer works.'

'That's very kind of you, but I wouldn't dream of taking up any of your time. Apart from that, I tend to make copious notes when I'm wandering around, and that would be most boring for a companion. But thanks for the offer.'

He removed his hand from my wrist, for my tone made my words sound like a snub. I bestowed a parting smile on him and left the dining room, keenly aware of a tingle running along my spine that came from the power of his blue eyes boring into my back.

I sighed heavily when I entered my room and closed the door. My knees suddenly seemed incapable of supporting me. Paul Russell had made quite an impact on me, and that was no mean feat for any man. I didn't have an ordinary job — I lived for my work, and there was no time for entanglements. Paul had summed me up correctly when he said I'd be wandering around with my head in the clouds and my imagination working overtime, for that was exactly how I lived. I had my own little dream world and was accustomed to guarding my privacy jealously. But I was aware that if any man could breach the walls of my ivory castle, it would be someone exactly like Paul Russell.

But he'd said he was an insurance agent! I shook my head slowly, using my acquired skill at characterisation. His name suited him but his job did not. I was pretty sure that when I wrote my next short story he would be the hero, and would have a glamorous livelihood.

My thoughts came down out of the clouds and I looked around the room, gripped by a harsh sense of cold reality. I envisioned a rabbit about to hop into a trap, and instinctively sensed that something bad was going to happen. I had intended to take a stroll on my first evening to get a glimpse of Rome and assimilate some of its atmosphere, but the discordant note in my mind was playing havoc with my nerves and I began to suffer a change of mind about leaving the hotel. Out there on the street, or perhaps now in the hotel, was the man who had paid to be informed of my arrival in Rome, and the moment I left this sanctuary some intangible contact would be made, the purpose of which I could not even begin to guess at.

I slid home the bolt on the door. I was tired and my nerve was failing. Tomorrow would be soon enough to expose myself, and by the morning, after a good night's rest, I might feel more sure of myself. But in my present state of mind, nothing could induce me to go out tonight.

There was some preparation work I could do. I needed to record my impressions of the journey over the last lap through northern Italy, and do it before the allure of Rome added its own overwhelming contribution of facts and dazzling sights to my crowded mind. I instinctively moved to the window to check on my car, and then noticed that my overnight bag was not on the floor by the bed where I had left it before going down to the dining room.

I halted in shock and looked around carefully. The bag was near the edge of the bed, zipped shut but with a scrap of pink lining showing. I certainly hadn't left it like that, and when I opened it I discovered that the lining was jammed in the zipper. Then I saw that the door of the wardrobe was ajar — but I could remember having turned the key in the lock.

The room had been entered during my sojourn in the dining room, and someone had looked through my possessions! A sense of revulsion filled me as I imagined unknown, disrespectful hands examining my treasured belongings. I opened one of my cases and saw that my notebooks had been disturbed. I use the standard reporter's notebooks, numbered on the front cover, and two of them were no longer in numerical order. I always kept them strictly in order, and this fact alone would have been sufficient to confirm my suspicion that the room had been searched.

I checked meticulously, but nothing was missing, so robbery had not been the motive. That fact scared me more than if I had returned and caught a thief red-handed. I experienced an uncanny sensation of being a fly trapped in a spider's web. It wasn't pleasant, and the icy tremors darting along my spine disconcerted me. Fear made me indecisive, which was uncharacteristic, and further demoralised me. I seemed to have been enveloped in the shrouds of a mystery, and the sooner I discovered what was going on, the better. That much was obvious, but how to unravel it was not so clear.

I dropped weakly onto the bed and

tried to reassure myself. But I was alone in a strange city, and some unknown person had an interest in me that I was afraid to guess at. I felt the situation close in on me and fought against it. What could I do? My mind would not function normally, and fear was tearing my composure to shreds.

A knock at the door startled me. I froze, gazing at the panels as if expecting a maniac to come bursting in. Then I heard Paul's voice outside, calm and firm, and I broke free from my unnerving fear and sprang to my feet. I was so pleased to hear his voice that forgot I had bolted the door when I tried to pull it open. My hand slid off the handle, which broke the nail on my little finger, and I cried out at the pain.

'Are you all right in there?' demanded Paul, rattling the handle.

I opened the door. He looked me up and down, his face showing concern.

'Sorry about that.' I forced a smile. 'I forgot that I'd bolted the door, and your knock startled me.' I checked the nail on my little finger, and he caught hold of my hand and inspected it.

'After you left me in the dining room,' he said, 'I got to thinking that you probably wouldn't start working today, so if you've a mind for some sight-seeing this evening then I'll be only too happy to show you around.' He was looking at me optimistically, and I was so relieved at his offer that I reached out and touched his forearm.

'Thank you, I'd love to,' I replied warmly. 'I certainly won't be doing any work this evening. In fact I was just thinking about what I should do later, but sight-seeing alone isn't much fun.'

'Tell me about it!' He smiled, his eyes shining. 'Hey, you didn't knock me back this time! Did I hear you right? You've agreed to go out with me this evening?'

He was the answer to a prayer, but I didn't tell him that. I smiled, feeling better already. 'I'll look forward to it,' I told him.

'Seven thirty?'

'I'll be ready.'

I realised that he was still holding my hand, and he squeezed my fingers gently as he departed. I watched him walk along the corridor to his room. His offer elated me; I wouldn't have much to fear while in his company. But as I closed the door, a thought came unbidden to my mind. Was Paul the mystery man who was interested in my movements, or was he what he appeared to be — a lonely holidaymaker who would appreciate some female company?

I stifled my doubts and spent the rest of the afternoon making plans for starting work the next day. Later I slept, for I had pushed myself on the last lap of the trip from England.

* * *

When I awoke, it was time for tea, and I looked for Paul in the dining room but he was not around. I returned to my room, a thrill of anticipation already burgeoning in my mind, and began checking the time every few moments, thinking that seven thirty would never come. But when I decided it was time to get myself ready, the time passed quickly. My favourite evening dress — on which I had splashed out recklessly in hopeful anticipation of some romantic evenings in Rome — was a pale-lemon creation, slightly flared at the knee, with thin straps that crossed at the back. I laid out some matching accessories and selected my jewellery, then attended to my hair. I decided to coil it at the side of my head but leave some tendrils loose, and I secured it with a diamante clip. Then I attached two small diamond shoulder clips to my dress that matched my hair clip. I slipped my feet into strappy shoes and picked up a matching clutch bag. The reflection which gazed back at me from the mirror was most pleasing, and I was satisfied that I looked my best.

Another glance at my watch informed me that it was now almost the appointed time. I was applying a final touch of lipstick when a knock came on the door.

I picked up my shrug, in case the evening turned cold, and, filled with rapidly growing anticipation, I opened the door to Paul.

3

His face lit up when he saw me, his lips rounding into a silent 'O' of appreciation at my appearance. His smile widened. My breath caught in my throat as I and noted his clean-cut figure, for here was one of my literary heroes in the flesh, looking as if he had just stepped out of the pages of my latest story to share my company. He whistled soundlessly.

'I wish I had a writer's mind,' he said softly. 'Then I could do justice to this vision before me.'

'And you've brushed up nicely too,' I observed. He was wearing a dark navy suit, his hair still damp from the shower.

'You've changed your manner as well as your clothes,' he remarked. 'When we met in the dining room you came across as somewhat . . . ' He paused to search for a word and smiled as he said, 'Prim? But obviously you were recovering from your journey to Rome, and immersed in thoughts of what you were planning to do.'

'First impressions aren't always the best,' I countered, laughing. 'When you saw me earlier I really was exhausted by the long drive. Plus, I've just finished a year or so of strenuous mental work, and my mind was still trying to sort out what I needed to learn about Rome in the two short weeks I have here. Now my plans are made and I'll begin working tomorrow. But tonight is mine, and I hope you have enough stamina to match my efforts to have a good time.'

'If that's the way you feel, then let's get started,' he challenged, his eyes glinting.

'I do like a bold, masterful man,' I countered.

He paused for the barest moment, his expression changing, and then he saw my smile and realised that I was bantering. He took my arm and led me out of the room, and at his touch all my cares and worries seemed to magically fall away. I cleared my mind completely, determined to have a good time. This was my night, come what may. With regard to the future, I mentally buried my head in the sand.

I was surprised to see a taxi waiting in the courtyard. Paul opened the door and we entered the vehicle. I leaned back against the upholstery with a sigh of relief and looked forward to the evening ahead. He had talked to the taxi driver before joining me, and I tingled as his thigh pressed against mine when he settled into the seat. Then the taxi drove out of the courtyard and we left the hotel.

'I've got the taxi for a couple of hours,' Paul remarked. 'You'll see the more popular tourist spots in comfort and decide which of them you'll want to check out on foot later.'

'That's thoughtful of you. A preview will save my steps.'

'I'd like to see some of your published work.'

'I haven't brought anything with me.

If you give me your home address, I'll send you something when I get back. In fact, you're such a good-looking man, I expect I'll write a short story with you as its hero.'

'Now that's something I should like to see!' He laughed.

'I do that all the time. Most of my friends have found their way into my stories — with different names, of course; but only I can recognise them.'

'And I suppose if people get on the wrong side of you, they end up as villains.'

Our laughter blended, and seemed to set the atmosphere between us for the evening. For my part, a strange and totally unknown mood seemed to envelop me, and I felt as if I was out of my body and watching myself acting in this light-hearted manner that had overtaken me. Perhaps it was because all my time was usually spent working with my nose to the grindstone, and now that I was relaxing I didn't quite know how to act. But it was a good feeling, and I liked it.

I had many opportunities to study Paul's profile as we proceeded. He had instructed the driver well, and during the next two hours we viewed most of the more popular tourist spots in Rome. My senses were overwhelmed by their beauty. I had to keep telling myself that this was not just some fantastic dream; that I really was on holiday in the Eternal City accompanied by the most gorgeous man I had ever met. I even made some mental notes about the places I could not afford to miss when I started working, and really enjoyed the company of this most attractive man whom Fate had placed at my disposal.

The taxi finally deposited us outside a night club, and Paul paid off the driver and turned to me, his smile wide and reassuring.

'This place is a must,' he explained. 'The food is out of this world, and the cabaret is excellent. This will be my second visit in two weeks, and I shall probably come again before my holiday ends — that's how good it is.'

He spoke with boyish fervour, and I could tell he was really enjoying himself because his habit of looking around occasionally as if expecting trouble was not in evidence.

The interior of the club was first-rate. Small tables were scattered around a central cleared space where couples were dancing. Several musicians were on the rear of a stage, and a female singer was in good voice. Subdued lighting was provided by table lamps that created an atmosphere of intimacy, and we sat close by the dance floor. There were some forty couples at the tables or dancing, and a buzz of excitement in the air quickly infected me.

'What would you like to drink?' Paul had to lean close to make himself heard. He looked ethereal in the pinkish glow of the lighting.

'A white wine with ice, please,' I replied, my fingers tapping the table in time with the song being sung.

Our drinks arrived. I sipped my refreshingly cold drink while Paul enjoyed a glass containing a red liquid. 'I'd like to dance before we eat,' he said.

'You might change your mind about that when I start stepping out,' I replied, getting to my feet. I saw his grimace as he followed me, but his fears soon vanished when we joined the couples on the floor and got into the rhythm of the music.

'You're a great dancer,' he whispered in my ear. 'You're making me feel like a cart horse.'

'I do believe you're fishing for a compliment,' I told him, and he laughed and held me closer.

From the moment he took me into his arms I was assailed by the most exquisite feelings. I felt like a teenager on her first date. My heart thudded and I felt light-headed. Paul was a good dancer, and I followed him intently until I could relax a little and begin to really enjoy the dance. I was slipping into a real holiday mood; and all thoughts of work, which had loomed large in my mind for weeks, faded away.

The nearness of Paul, his strong arms holding me close, was the closest thing to heaven I had ever experienced. I felt safe with him, and he did not seem like a stranger as we moved easily around the floor. I leaned against him, feeling his heat. This was better than working, I thought, and began to wish the evening would never end.

We went back to the table and ordered a meal. Afterwards I could not recall exactly what it was I ate, but it was delicious. We danced again and again, and I felt as if I could go on forever. If this was a sample of what my holiday would be like, then the next two weeks would be a whirl of joy. My mind was cleared completely of the nagging of work that had to be done. I was enjoying myself for the first time in many months. It was like being released from prison, and I relished it.

'It's almost midnight,' Paul said at length, and his words brought me crashing down to earth like Cinderella at the ball. 'I could go on like this all night,' he continued, 'but I'm aware that you're a working woman and may want to be out researching at the crack of dawn. Do you want to call it a day?'

'Can't we carry on a while yet?' I whispered, looking up into his face. He was smiling. The subdued lighting enhanced his looks, and he seemed almost of another world. His left hand gently squeezed my shoulder.

'I could certainly make it to dawn,' he replied. 'You're the one to be considered, so just say the word.'

Reality was like a cold blast from the arctic. But we were no longer strangers. A kind of rapport existed between us now. I nodded slowly, and the only thought in my mind was the anticipation of being kissed goodnight by this divine man.

'We'd better go,' I said reluctantly, 'although I don't want to. I can't remember ever having as good a time as this before.'

'But all good things must come to an end,' he said.

I seemed to slip into a lower gear as we departed, the music still ringing in my ears. Paul got a taxi and we sped back to the hotel. My mind slipped back into its usual rut and became partially submerged under the weight of what I had planned for my holiday. But nothing could detract from the fine feeling of happiness inside me. I knew I'd never forget my first evening out with a living literary hero.

There was a light showing at the hotel entrance. 'That doesn't look very inviting after the night club,' I remarked as we alighted from the taxi.

Paul took my arm and we entered the hotel. For once, the receptionist was not at her desk; and thinking about her as we went up to our rooms, I wondered what little game of intrigue she was playing. But I was too elated by the pleasure of the evening to dwell on the unknown. When we reached my door, I turned to Paul to thank him for the evening, and he surprised me by pulling me into his arms.

My mouth was half-open as I started to speak, but his lips cut off my words and nature took control. I had been wondering all evening what it would be like to be kissed by this handsome man, and I was not disappointed. The touch of his lips sent a shiver through me and I thought of a violin being handled by a maestro. Paul's arms enclosed me and his lips took possession of my mouth. I closed my eyes, and might have fallen if he had not been holding me tightly. I could not tell if I was on my head or my heels. Time stood still. Sensation filled me. I had been kissed many times, but this . . . I did not want it to end, but Paul's lips finally withdrew and I gasped for breath.

'Goodnight, Gail,' he said huskily. 'I've had a wonderful time. See you tomorrow. Sleep well.'

He departed, leaving me standing at

the door. My senses seemed to be whirling, and for a few moments my balance was faulty. Then I calmed down sufficiently to unlock my door. When I went to bed, it was a long time before I fell asleep.

* * *

Daylight peeping in at the window awakened me, and as soon as I opened my eyes my thoughts went back over every fleeting moment of the previous evening. I tingled as I relived the pleasure of Paul's kiss. Then I thought of all the things I planned to do today and arose eagerly. The day was beautiful; bright sunlight was streaming in through the open window and small, fleecy white clouds adorned a perfect blue sky. I looked down at my car, and was reassured by the sight of it standing exactly where I had left it.

I showered and then prepared for my morning excursion, donning a blue cotton dress with short sleeves. I checked my watch and realised it was too early to go down to the dining room, but I was impatient to see Paul again, and wondered how he was reviewing our evening together. Would he be as enthusiastic about it as I? I had never felt like this before, and realised that I would have to calm down if I was go about my business today as I had planned.

I began to reconsider the incidents that had occurred the day before. They were simple to sum up. There was Paul, my only contact in Rome. Had our meeting been as casual as it seemed? I didn't like the thought that he might have been playing a role the previous evening. My instincts insisted that I couldn't possibly be wrong about him. I didn't dare let my doubts take on substance, for that would entail disengaging from him, and I liked him very much. But if he was the man the receptionist had telephoned, then I ought to have nothing to do with him.

After more consideration, I decided to skip breakfast to avoid bumping into him. He would probably be in the dining room waiting for me to appear, so I decided I could get something to eat later. But I was becoming exasperated by the situation that seemed to be building up around me, for I wanted nothing to spoil my holiday.

While I was dithering, there was a knock at the door. My heart lurched as I moistened my lips, and the knock was repeated before I finally went forward to open the door. Paul was standing there, a big smile on his handsome face, and my pulse slipped into a higher gear.

'Good morning,' he greeted me. 'I'm on my way down to breakfast and thought you might like some company. How are you feeling after last night? You certainly made a fine start to your holiday. I had to make a real effort to keep up with you. I don't know about you, but I certainly enjoyed myself. It was by far the best evening I've had here so far.'

'I thoroughly enjoyed last night,' I replied. 'It was a perfect introduction to the city. But I was planning to miss breakfast, as I want to get started on my work programme.'

'My dear woman, you'll find eating out expensive unless you know where to go. Apart from that, trudging around Rome is hard work, and you'll need a good breakfast inside you to stave off the dreaded mid-morning gap.' His firm tone undermined my determination to put my nose to the grindstone, for I was hungry, and he was very much a sociable character.

'You sound just like my mother!' I laughed, and he joined in. 'All right, you've talked me into it. Let's go down to breakfast.'

We were still laughing when we entered the dining room, and something had happened to me in the few moments since he had knocked on my door. I felt at ease and contented — the desperate urge to be in his company again had subsided now that we were together. During the meal he broached the subject of my plans.

'I'd welcome the chance of some more of your company,' he said hopefully. 'It is tiresome being alone all the time, and the sound of your voice is inviting.'

'I'm in two minds about what I should do. I don't really feel like starting work just yet. I expect I'm still tired from the journey. My plan is to visit the Spanish Steps this morning, sight-see like an ordinary holidaymaker, and make notes later from memory. So if you really feel like joining me, then I'd be glad of your company.'

'I accept your offer,' he said quickly. 'Just say where you want to go and I'll convey you on my magic carpet.'

I smiled, but I was wondering where my resolve had disappeared to. I really wanted to be in his company, and I was aware that if we did not spend more time together I should be disappointed for the rest of the day.

'The Spanish Steps first,' I decided, 'and you can leave the magic carpet behind this morning because we can easily walk there.'

He nodded, his eyes glinting in a way that turned my knees to jelly. He really was the most handsome man I had ever met, and already I was half-wishing there hadn't been any of that mysterious business the evening before. If ever a man was born for a holiday romance, it was Paul Russell.

By the time we finished breakfast I was bubbling with anticipation. We returned to my room to collect my shoulder bag and camera, and I ensured that I had a notebook and at least two pens, although I didn't think I would write a single word when there was so much enjoyment and pleasure to be experienced.

The receptionist was at her desk in the lobby when we passed, and she looked up with a strange little half-smile on her lips. 'Enjoy your day,' she called, and I forced a carefree smile as we departed with a casual wave. When I paused in the doorway and glanced back at her, she was reaching for the telephone, and I wondered if she was about to warn someone that the fox had left its lair.

I felt like an escaped prisoner, and stayed very close to Paul as we walked along the teeming streets. With my 35mm camera slung over one shoulder and my bag over the other, I looked no different from any of the other tourists roaming around. But I certainly felt different. There was a leaping exultation inside me because I was with Paul, and I did not stop to wonder why I should react in this manner. He had that effect on me, and I was not going to look a gift horse in the mouth.

Our surroundings filled me with wonder and I did not know where to look first as we walked. I tried to take in the sights and memorise them for future reference. We reached the Corso, which led directly into the Piazza di Spagna, and turned left into the Via Condotti. I kept stopping to look in the windows of the many shops selling luxury goods of all kinds, and Paul waited patiently, smiling good-naturedly. We emerged from the Via Condotti to enter the Piazza di Spagna, and there directly before us were the famous Spanish Steps.

As a writer, I ought to have been able to take in the scene unemotionally; to record it professionally for future use. It was breathtaking, and I gazed enraptured at the seemingly endless steps and the church that overlooked them. It had two towers, each surmounted by a cross, and there was a clock in the left-hand tower. The steps, a splendid baroque stairway, curved in a horseshoe from the terrace outside the church and around a second terrace massed with colourful azaleas, then broadened out into the square where I was standing. I was surprised to see innumerable paintings, some on easels and others propped on the steps; each, while awaiting a buyer, adding its own magic to the vivid scene.

My writer's mind immediately began to form descriptive sentences and a story plot. I imagined a heroine standing here for the first time. A handsome hero, Paul Russell, would be about to introduce himself, and I nodded thoughtfully as I appraised him. This holiday was going to be fruitful in many ways.

'Quite beautiful, isn't it?' he said. He was smiling, obviously enamoured by the scene. 'This definitely is one of my favourite views.'

'I've never seen anything so beautiful,' I replied. 'I'm going to have to make some notes now. I can't rely on memory — afterthought would never do justice to the scene.'

'Sure, go ahead. Sit down over there in the shade. I won't disturb you.'

I spent twenty minutes scribbling on a pad, glancing up at the scene repeatedly to get all the details. When I had finished, Paul came to sit by my side, his knee against my thigh. I experienced the most exquisite reaction, shivering as the pleasure of our contact swept through me.

'There are a lot of facts I could tell you about some of these sights,' he said. 'It would save you doing masses of research, which must be quite time-consuming.' His blue eyes shone in the sunlight.

'Not today,' I said, getting to my feet. 'It's holiday time, remember?'

His laughter rang in my ears, and then I halted so quickly that he bumped against me, almost knocking me off my feet. His hands lifted with commendable speed and flashed out to grasp my elbows.

I clutched at him to maintain my balance, but my attention was fixed on a stocky little man standing some yards away, partially concealed by the crowd milling around. I recognised him immediately as the fellow that had been looking at my car in the hotel courtyard the day before. He was regarding me intently, and a cold shiver ran down my spine.

'That man!' I gasped, pointing him out. 'He was trying to steal my car last night!'

'What?' Paul's face was a study in shock. 'What man?'

'Do you see the man in the brown shirt and beige trousers? Look! He's making off!'

'Wait here. I'll get him.' Paul darted off, but the Italian had already vanished into the crowd. My hero-figure did likewise, and I frowned as they were both lost to sight.

I was shocked by the stocky man's appearance, for I knew his turning up was not a coincidence. He must have been following me; had probably been outside the hotel waiting for me to emerge. I stood motionless for what seemed an eternity before Paul returned, breathing heavily. His handsome face was grim as he gazed at me.

'I couldn't catch him,' he reported. 'He had too good a start, and got away in the crowd. You said he tried to steal your car?'

I explained the incident in the hotel courtyard and also mentioned that my room had been entered and searched. I watched Paul's face for his reaction.

'I don't like the sound of this.' He shook his head. 'He must have followed you from the hotel. Why didn't you tell me about this yesterday?'

'I didn't know you from Adam yesterday,' I said shakily.

'This should be reported to the police.'

'No. I'm sure they would just waste a great deal of my time. I don't need to get caught up in something like that.' I paused and watched his face, thinking how open and honest his blue eyes seemed. He was genuinely concerned about me, and now kept looking around, probably wondering what would happen next.

'I'll see that no harm comes to you,' he said resolutely, a harsh expression showing in his eyes.

I nodded slowly. 'That's kind of you.'

'I'm delighted to be of service. You look quite shaken, Gail. Let's get a drink. I know a nice little place across the piazza. Come on, a cup of coffee will do you good.'

He grasped my elbow and steered me through the crowd, and I felt comforted by the contact. The café was filled with tourists eating gelato or drinking coffee, though there were some locals present. Paul found a corner table, and when I accidently bumped a woman's shoulder as I squeezed into my seat I apologised, and she replied in what I recognised to be German.

'Sorry about the crush, but it's like this all over Rome,' Paul observed. 'You'll get used to it by your second week. Perhaps for a working holiday, you should have come in the off-season.'

'No, I needed to come in the peak season to capture the atmosphere and the sunshine.'

A waitress brought coffee, and I grimaced at its taste, finding it very strong. Paul noticed and smiled. His powerful gaze disconcerted me.

'You're worried, aren't you?' he asked quietly. 'That man has upset you. Why don't you let me talk to the police about him? I saw him and can give a description. They might keep a watch around the hotel to see if he shows up there again.'

'It might be nothing at all,' I replied, wanting to believe it. 'I'm not Italian, and there is a certain type of local male who is interested only in foreigners.'

'That depends on what their business is,' he replied gravely. 'But as you'll be sight-seeing instead of working today, I suggest a bit of exploration. Like any other city, but more so in Rome, you can only do justice to the sights by travelling on foot. I've already done the rounds, and one of the most charming corners I've discovered is the Aventine Hill. We'll have to take a bus to avoid climbing it, but you'll be well pleased with the view.'

'Anything you say.' I felt so unnerved that I was ready to agree to any suggestion he made so long as he stayed with me.

We caught a bus, and on entering I was surprised to see the conductor on a kind of throne. Paul paid the fare, and we finally alighted at the top of the hill. There were other tourists, a fact that relieved me because I felt safer with people around, although no one would trouble me while Paul was with me. He looked like a man who could take care of himself.

'There you are,' he declared as we entered a park with a terrace overlooking the Tiber. 'That's Trastevere across the river, and beyond that the Janiculum Hill.'

'I'll have to look them up in my guide book,' I replied, and he smiled and clasped my hand as I reached into my shoulder bag.

'Not today. This is a sight-seeing trip, remember? There's a statue of Garibaldi on the Janiculum Hill, but you can see that another time, perhaps when you visit the Vatican.'

'You've certainly done your homework.' I smiled, and his blue eyes sparkled as our gazes met and held. I could feel trust forming a base in the background of my mind. I had an instinctive feeling that I might need a friend before my holiday was over, and he had told me that his holiday would end about the same time that mine did. If he found pleasure escorting me around, then I'd not complain.

He pointed to a quiet, tree-shaded road and we walked along it until it opened out into yet another piazza. 'What place is this?' I asked.

'It's the Piazza dei Cavalieri di Malta.' He smiled as he led me to a gateway on the right-hand side. 'Just take a look through that keyhole.'

I did so, and was enthralled to see, perfectly framed in the keyhole, the Church of St Peter's in the distance.

'How beautiful!' I whispered.

'Everything in Rome is beautiful,' he replied gently. 'Now you should see the rose gardens. There are more than five thousand bushes.'

'Have you taken a course in how to be a guide in Rome?' I asked him with a smile.

He laughed. 'I prepared myself by reading everything that's been written about it.'

I glanced at my watch as a pang of hunger stabbed me, and he consulted his too, nodding. 'Time has flown. But that's the way it goes in Rome. If you're as ready to eat as I am, then I suggest we either return to the hotel or visit a trattoria. I learned my mistake when I first arrived. It's best to pick out a café that looks clean and has plenty of Italian customers.'

'I'll leave it to you,' I responded, feeling tired and overheated. 'Although I think it might be better to return to the hotel. I've done enough walking for my first day, and seeing that little man earlier gave me quite a shock. Plus I have a splitting headache.'

'I'm sorry for not being more considerate,' he said instantly. 'The glare of the sun is probably affecting you. Come on, I'll take you back to the hotel. You can rest up this afternoon, and if you're feeling better this evening I'll be happy to take you out and show you more Roman night-life.'

'That's kind of you. But you'll have to work really hard to show me a better time than I had last evening.' I paused and put a hand on his arm. 'I've really appreciated your company this morning.'

My shock at seeing the stocky Italian was wearing off, and I was looking at Paul in a different light. Naturally I had suspected his motives because he had been the first man to make contact with me after my arrival. But I was a great one for relying on instinct, and I felt in my heart that he was genuine — although I could not picture him as being someone in insurance. It was the only fact about him that jarred, and I put that down to my sense of the romantic.

He was really handsome and ought to have had a glamorous job — an airline pilot or something like that. But again, that impression stemmed from my writer's mind. Show me a handsome man and there is no limit to the daydreams I can weave around him.

When we reached the hotel, the receptionist greeted us cordially. In my present mood I was ready to believe the worst of her, for she held the key to the whole mystery. But I could not broach the subject because it would only put her on her guard.

'Mr Russell,' she said, 'you have a message. Your Rome office wants you to call in.'

'Oh, Lord!' He shook his head ruefully

and grimaced. 'That's the worst of being in my line of business, and I made the mistake of letting them know I was coming to Rome on holiday. Still, if I handle this successfully I might get transferred here. That would certainly be a bonus.'

'You've only been here two weeks and already you're lonely,' I said, and he grinned.

'Working here would be different. But I'd better go and talk to them. Being in your company has made me forget that I had to check with the office. That's Rome for you! But it's a good thing we haven't made arrangements for this afternoon. It would have been a pity to disappoint you. I do hope your headache will ease, and I'll check with you later.'

'You are not feeling well?' the receptionist asked.

'It's mainly excitement,' I replied. 'I'll get over it. I'm just not accustomed to the exercise.'

'Your meal will be served if you go into the dining room,' she advised me.

Paul took his leave and I went in to

lunch. After the meal I went up to my room and stood at the window, studying the small section of the street that I could see, and some moments elapsed before I realised that I was instinctively looking for the elusive Italian. I turned away from the window, vowing not to let the situation worry me. If I ever came face to face with that little man I'd give him a good piece of my mind. I was not going to permit him to spoil my holiday!

The afternoon lay before me, unplanned because Paul had been called away. Considering the events of the morning, I realised that some reorganisation of my agenda was necessary. I would be exhausted very quickly if I walked everywhere, so I'd have to use the car to survey the city in order to select the sights worthy of further exploration. I decided to spend the afternoon doing this.

When I reached the lobby on my way out, the receptionist called to me from her desk. I went across, gazing into her dark, expressionless eyes, wondering what it was she knew that I didn't. I wished I could have read her mind.

'It is so nice that you have made friends with Mr Russell,' she said. 'It's a pity he cannot accompany you this afternoon.'

'He seems to be a nice type, but I'm on a working holiday and I'll be using my car this afternoon.'

'You may find parking difficult. Are you going anywhere in particular?'

My eyes narrowed as I considered, but I managed to maintain an expressionless face, for her gaze was intent.

'Not really. I'll drive around looking at the sights, and make a selection of those I wish to visit on foot. That should save a lot of time.'

'How is your headache now? I noticed that you were not wearing sunglasses this morning, and that could have affected you.'

'It's much better, thank you.' I checked my shoulder bag and camera and departed, glancing around casually to see if the mysterious little Italian was anywhere in the vicinity, but did not spot him.

I felt safer in the car, and drove along the route I had noted on my street plan. I soon discovered that Rome did have traffic problems, and parking would certainly be difficult. I also discovered that checking landmarks from a moving car was extremely difficult, but I glimpsed the Colosseum, then cut through a number of smaller streets and followed the traffic in a northerly direction, wanting to locate the Villa Borghese.

I passed a large railway station, keeping one eye on the road and the other on my surroundings, but it was a dangerous way to drive under prevailing conditions, and I began to think that it would better to enlist Paul's aid. He could drive the car while I took in the sights.

A car suddenly sped by and cut closely in front of me. I am a cautious driver and always allow the regulation distance between myself and the vehicle in front, but even so I was forced to brake, and the Corsa screeched to a halt. The road hog darted away even before I stopped, and if I had not made an emergency stop there would have been a collision.

My gaze lifted to the rear-view mirror, for tyres were screeching on the road behind, and I gasped in horror when I saw a large red Fiat bearing down on me. I just had time to put the car out of gear before he hit me with a sickening thud of buckling metal. If it wasn't for my seat belt I would certainly have been injured, and I sat gripping the steering wheel as the series of metal-rending sounds and shattering glass faded into a frightening silence, and I sat trembling, shocked and bewildered.

4

The driver of the Fiat was apparently unhurt. I sat motionless in my seat and watched him get out of his car. He was tall, dark and handsome, dressed in a lightweight pale blue suit and a red necktie. I judged that he was about thirty years old. He came quickly to my car, jerked open my door while I fumbled with my seat belt, and bent to look in at me, his dark eyes filled with concern.

'Are you all right?' he asked me. 'Are you hurt?'

'I don't think so,' I replied, trying to recover from my shock. 'Did you see that road hog?' I alighted from the car, staggered, and he grasped my arm.

'Take it easy,' he advised, taking in my pale face with narrowed brown eyes. His long hair was black and crinkled into tight waves. His bronzed face was strong-featured, with jutting brows and a good chin. His lips curved sensually as he smiled at me, trying to make light of the accident. 'That maniac should be put behind bars. But let us look at the cars. I think mine came off worse than yours.'

He took hold of my arm and walked to the back of my car, taking me with him. I was horrified to see my rear bumper was badly bent and the boot lid was twisted out of line. The rear lights were broken. But his car had taken more damage. The front bumper was bent, the headlights smashed and the nearside wing crumpled.

'I didn't get his number,' I said unsteadily.

'I didn't either.' He pulled a face.

'You're speaking English!' I exclaimed. My mind was beginning to function normally again. In the background the traffic was continuing along the street as if nothing had happened. We were out of the general stream and they just drove around us, nobody much interested in just another road incident. 'How did you know I'm English?'

'Your GB plate on the back,' he said. 'It was all I could see as I slid toward you. My name is Donato di Barocci.'

'I'm Gail Bennett.' My voice was unsteady, laced with shock. 'What do we do now?'

'Nobody has been injured, so there is no need to report the matter to the police. I ran into you when you braked, so I was not keeping a proper distance from you. I accept full responsibility for the damage to your car. My apologies! I hope you were not going anywhere in a hurry. But I can deal with this quite easily. Fortunately, my father is a businessman, and among his properties there is a large garage. Just wait here in case a policeman arrives and I'll go and telephone our garage to bring another car and some help to take our vehicles away.'

He bent to examine my rear wheels, then walked around the car to check all round before looking at his own vehicle.

He was nodding as he came back to me. 'They can both be driven under their own power,' he said. 'That is good.'

'Then I'll drive my car to a garage,' I said, aware that a small crowd was gathering on a nearby pavement.

'But I will pay for the damage that has been done,' he insisted, 'and it will be much cheaper if the repairs are carried out at my father's garage.' He paused and looked into my eyes. 'You are shocked by what has happened, and you shouldn't drive in that condition. Wait here and I'll get help.'

I was still feeling shaky and nodded reluctantly in agreement. I watched his tall figure as he walked away along the hot pavement. Some of the crowd began to drift away. And I was appalled by the lack of interest that had been shown. I leaned against my car, aware that my legs were trembling, and within a few moments di Barocci returned, an expansive smile on his dark features.

'It's all been arranged,' he told me. 'Help is on its way.' He gazed ruefully at his own car. 'That has only just been repaired. Two teenagers stole it three weeks ago and did considerable damage while joyriding. My father will insist that I start walking in future.'

'But it wasn't your fault any more than it was mine,' I said quickly. 'That maniac who cut in front of me was to blame.'

He produced a gold cigarette case and held it out to me. I declined. I have never smoked, and although my nerves were badly shaken I had no intention of starting a bad habit. He selected a cigarette, put it between his lips, and produced a beautiful gold lighter. As blue smoke drifted away he looked at me again. I liked his voice, which sounded musical yet husky. He would be another good candidate for the hero in one of my future romance stories.

'Have you been in Rome long?' he asked.

'I arrived yesterday. Not a very good start to a holiday, is it?'

'You don't really need a car here. It is

much easier to get around without one.'

'That much I have already discovered!' I smiled ruefully.

We talked generally while waiting. He asked where I was staying and for how long. Then a cream Fiat drew up behind his car and two men got out, one of them wearing a mechanic's overalls. They came forward, and Donato spoke rapidly in Italian, explaining what had happened. When he glanced at me I feigned indifference, as if I did not understand the language. I was not about to let anyone in Rome know that I could speak and understand Italian.

'What I've arranged is to use the car they've brought and take you to wherever you want to go. They will take our cars to my father's garage and commence work on the repairs. Is that all right by you?'

'Certainly. I'll just get my bag and camera from the car. But shouldn't we try to trace that other driver? If we can't claim against his insurance for the damage, he should at least be charged with dangerous driving.'

He laughed. 'Don't worry about it! By now he's probably on the other side of Rome, judging by the speed he was doing. Did you get a look at him? Could you describe his car to the police?'

I shook my head. 'He was gone too quickly for that. It was a red car, but I can't even say what make. I didn't get a look at the driver either.' A sigh gusted through me as I shook my head helplessly.

He shrugged his shoulders fatalistically. 'It could be worse. Get your things and I'll drive you back to your hotel, if you like.'

'But what about you?' I insisted. 'You weren't just driving idly around, were you? This has interrupted your business.'

'Not at all! I've just returned from Florence and I'm taking a few days off from business. I place myself at your service, and if you require a knowledgeable guide to show you around Rome then you could not have bumped into a more qualified person.'

'*You* bumped into *me*,' I reminded him, and he laughed, his face cheerful, his brown eyes gleaming in the sunlight.

'Take away the cars,' he told the two garage men, and I went to my Vauxhall and collected my belongings.

We stood and watched the two cars being driven away, and then Donato ushered me to the waiting Fiat. I sat in the front passenger seat and fastened the seat belt, and he did the same as he slid behind the wheel.

'Well, now you can sit back and relax. You couldn't see much of the sights, could you, driving in traffic and trying to look around.'

'I had just arrived at that conclusion when you ran into me,' I replied.

'So I am an answer to your prayers.' A smile curved his sensual lips, and I nodded thoughtfully. He had certainly come along at the right moment, and I felt a prickle of anticipation shiver through me as I studied his handsome profile. He had a commanding way about him, as if he was accustomed to giving orders and having them obeyed without question. But he was not imperious, and I liked him instinctively from the outset. He had shown amazingly fast reactions in stopping his car when I made my emergency stop without warning.

'Were you going anywhere in particular?' he asked softly, breaking into my thoughts.

'Not really. I was just looking over the ground, so to speak. I shall visit the Colosseum during the week, and I was actually trying to locate the Villa Borghese.'

'Why don't you place yourself in my hands?' he suggested. 'I am at a loose end for a few days. And it would give me great pleasure to show you around. I should like to be able to prove to you that not all Italians are maniacs.' He laughed, revealing perfect teeth, his heavy-lidded eyes blinking swiftly. As he looked at me, I could not see anything to dislike either in his appearance or his manner.

'I'm here on a working holiday,' I said.

'That sounds interesting. I am the world's greatest listener, so tell me about yourself.' As he spoke he swung the car expertly around another road hog who was edging out from a side street, and I clenched my teeth until the danger was past, but he showed no signs of anxiety and smiled easily. 'One becomes accustomed to this way of life,' he explained.

'What do you do for a living?' I asked.

'I asked you that question first,' he cut in. 'You mentioned a working holiday, and that intrigues me. Don't you have enough money to get back to England?'

'It isn't that kind of working holiday.' I smiled as I settled back in my seat and gave him a potted history of myself. He listened intently, and when I lapsed into silence threw me a shrewd glance.

'You are an astonishing woman. How

very clever to be able to do that sort of thing! I am most interested. You must tell me exactly how you work.'

His words sounded familiar, and I felt guilty as I recalled Paul Russell. But something mysterious and strange was happening around the hotel, and I found the company of this complete stranger refreshing.

'What about you?' I asked. 'How is it you speak impeccable English?'

'I've spent a lot of time in England. My father has business interests in London. I have travelled all over the world, and I speak five languages.'

'Languages were never my strong point,' I said, still feeling coy about my ability to speak Italian. Having denied any knowledge of the language, I was not about to change horses in midstream.

'But you must be excellent at English, which is the most difficult language in the world to master, is it not?'

I explained about my father, and saw Donato's face take on a shadow of sympathy. His bronzed features were so expressive. I sensed that he was really sorry for me, and yet we were but mere strangers thrown together by accident.

'I don't get the time to read, but to be able to write! Now that really must be something! You should feel very proud of yourself.' He paused. 'Gail. May I call you Gail?' He glanced at me, and I nodded. 'That's a very pretty name. You must call me Donato. Now, look ahead. We are driving along the Via Isonzo. When we turn into the Via Pinciano you'll see the Villa Borghese slightly to the right. I would like to walk you along the Avenue of the Magnolias, which leads to the Villa Borghese, which has the largest park in Rome. Perhaps tomorrow we will visit. There is a zoo in the park. But what can I tell you about the Borghese, eh?'

He paused for a moment to concentrate on his driving. I looked around with mounting eagerness. 'Is that the Galleria Borghese?' I asked, indicating the stark outline of a large building showing in the background amidst some trees.

'That's right. It was planned by Cardinal Borghese and built to house a museum. It belongs to the nation now and is one of the most important collections of Italian art, particularly of the seventeenth and eighteenth centuries.' He smiled at me, the corners of his eyes crinkling. 'Do I sound like a guidebook?'

'No. Please tell me more. I need all the facts I can get.' Enthusiasm bubbled over in my tone.

'I can tell that you are a true art lover! I shall bring you here tomorrow. That is, unless you have made other arrangements?' He raised an eyebrow at me, and I quickly shook my head. He nodded. 'That is good. Just wait until you see the Gallery of the Emperors! You must tell me exactly what you wish to see in Rome, and I will spirit you there as if by a magic carpet.'

I laughed lightly, the shock of the accident receding from my mind under his gentle friendliness. All that had occurred before our meeting now seemed unreal to me, and I relaxed completely for the first time since seeing the stocky little Italian snooping around my car and hearing the hotel receptionist's telephone conversation.

We continued, and Donato miraculously found a place to park. We left the Fiat and went to a nearby café that was off the tourist track and not unduly crowded. There were several tables covered with bright check cloths set outside on the wide pavement, but only five people were seated there. We went inside, where it was cool and there was no glare from the sun. There were more tables in the long room, and a bar before the back wall.

'Let us sit there.' Donato indicated a corner table. 'I know the couple that run this place and it is always quiet and clean.'

'Not at all like the café I visited this morning near the Spanish Steps,' I said, repressing a shudder as I recalled the black coffee.

A short, plump woman, aged about thirty, came through a doorway in the back wall. I leaned back in my seat, appreciating the cool atmosphere. Outside, the temperature was well up in the twenties.

'Ah, Donato!' exclaimed the woman, and he cut in swiftly, speaking English.

'Carlotta, come and meet an Englishwoman. We were involved in a minor accident earlier.' His eyes gleamed as he watched the woman coming around the counter. She had black hair and olive skin. Her eyebrows were finely arched and her lips curved into a smile as she halted by the table. 'Gail, this is Carlotta. She is the wife of a very good friend of mine. She speaks excellent English. How long were you in England, Carlotta?'

'Four years,' she replied, smiling at me. 'I'm pleased to meet you, Gail.'

'How do you do?' I replied, and Donato laughed.

'That's as English as you can get,' he observed. 'It is a phrase I've often wondered about. When one is introduced to an English person the greeting is always, 'How do you do?' And the answer is always the same — 'How do you do?''

'You did say English is the most difficult language to understand,' I returned.

'What would you like to drink?' asked Carlotta in an attractive, low-pitched tone. Her dark eyes seemed almost black, but she had a friendly, homely expression, and seemed to be just the right person to be running a café.

'No coffee, thank you,' I said quickly. 'A nice, long, cool drink would be like nectar.'

'Orange or lemon?'

'I think orange would hit the spot, please.'

'I'll have a granite di caffe,' Donato said.

'What on earth is that?' I asked, playing my part as a tourist who had no knowledge of Italian.

'Black coffee steeped in crushed ice and topped with whipped cream,' Carlotta responded. 'I'll put some ice in your orange, Gail.'

'Thank you.' I smiled. It was nice to hear my name on her lips and to feel secure in Donato's company. He was leaning back in his chair, watching me intently, and when our glances met he smiled.

'What is wrong with your boyfriend that he should let you come alone on holiday?' he asked me.

'I don't have a boyfriend. In my line of work there is never any time for socialising.'

'The English have a saying about all work and no play,' he countered.

'That applies to some people, but my job is not an ordinary one. It's more a way of life.'

Carlotta returned with a tray and set a cup of coffee before Donato and a tall glass of orange juice in front of me. I hadn't realised just how parched I was until I saw the juice, and sipped it gratefully.

'You said something about an accident,' Carlotta prompted.

'Some idiot cut in front of Gail and she made an emergency stop right in front of me,' Donato said, and I shivered at the recollection of that near disaster.

'It's a good thing you have the reactions of a cat,' I told him. 'I looked in my rear-view mirror and saw you coming towards me, and I could only put the car out of gear so that I'd roll when you hit me.'

'That was quick thinking,' he commended me, 'just as your emergency stop was a credit to your driving.'

A bell rang outside, and Carlotta suppressed a sigh as she went to answer it, shaking her head. Donato watched her through narrowed eyes, then glanced at me and saw that I was watching him.

'We were all at school together,' he said, smiling. 'Carlotta, and Carlo, her husband. I helped them raise the money to buy this place. It is a good living, but one is always at the beck and call of the customers. It would not suit me.'

'They don't appear to be very busy,' I ventured. 'Is it always this quiet?'

'No. They do a good evening trade. I think we'll visit the Villa Borghese tomorrow afternoon. I'm sure you'd like to drive around the avenues in a horse cab before looking through the museum. Then we'll drop in here and spend the evening. Would you like that?'

'It sounds fine. But I must do some work.'

'All right. Work in the morning. I shall have some business to handle before noon, but I'll be free after that. I'll see to it that you'll have a holiday to remember.'

'You're being very kind!'

'Not at all. The accident is down to me. I should not have been driving so close to you.'

'We were fortunate that it didn't turn out much worse.'

'It couldn't have turned out better,' he countered with a smile. 'It brought us into contact. We shall see Rome together. Although I live in the city, there are many places of interest I have never had the time to visit. If you will permit, we'll visit them now.'

'I've made a list of the places I really must make a point of seeing to get some notes down on paper,' I explained.

'I am very good at mixing business with pleasure, so we shall have the best of both worlds.'

I drank my juice and felt much refreshed. Carlotta was busy for some minutes with customers at the tables on the pavement. Donato drank his coffee, and an air of intimacy seemed to close in around us.

'I'll let you have the use of the Fiat until your own car has been repaired,' he said suddenly. 'You may need a vehicle, for it will be at least a week before yours is back on the road.'

'Will it cost a great deal to be repaired?' I asked doubtfully.

'Think nothing of it. I'll drive you to your hotel. I can take a taxi from there.'

I nodded, aware that it wold be useless to argue with him, and we took our leave of Carlotta, Donato promising to return with me the next evening.

When we were back in the car he glanced at me. 'What hotel are you staying at?' he asked.

I told him and fastened my seat belt as he drove on, enjoying his company, and sensing that it might prove to be advantageous having him around, because the moment I reached the hotel I would walk back into the centre of a mystery.

When we reached the hotel he parked in the courtyard and we alighted. I was aware that the receptionist was watching us from just inside the doorway, and a prickling sensation travelled up and down my spine. Donato dropped the keys of the Fiat into my palm and smiled as I started to protest again.

'Don't say it,' he urged. 'There is no need. At what time may I call for you tomorrow afternoon?'

'I shall visit the Colosseum in the morning. Shall we meet at two thirty?'

'That will be fine. I must warn you that I am a very punctual person. I'll be here right on the dot.'

'Thank you so much.' I held out my

hand, and for a moment my fingers were held tightly in his cool grasp. I looked into his dark eyes and felt a pang of some undefinable emotion stab through me. He smiled, his teeth startlingly white in his tanned face.

'Until tomorrow,' he said.

I watched him as he walked out of the courtyard, and he hailed a taxi and got into it. He smiled and waved as he was borne away, and when he was gone I felt tension begin to fill me. I drew a deep breath and walked into the hotel to find Paul standing at the desk, chatting with the receptionist.

'Hello,' he greeted me. He had been talking rapidly in Italian until I appeared. 'So you recovered from your headache and went out. But where's your car? You haven't let some back-street dealer talk you into exchanging it, have you?'

'No, I haven't.' I began to explain the whole sequence of events, feeling annoyance at his peremptory tone. He seemed to think that I could not be trusted out alone on the streets of Rome. But his expression changed as I told him about the accident, and concern showed on his strong features. I could not help comparing him to Donato, and at that moment I could not tell which of them I liked most.

'Were you hurt?' he asked, looking me over, a frown marring his forehead. 'I told you it wasn't safe on the streets.'

'I'm all right. But it was a close thing. Thank heaven Donato is a decent type.'

'Donato?' Paul queried.

'Donato di Barocci. It was his car that ran into me.'

'And you're on first-name terms with him?' There was a tight note in Paul's tone that made me glance swiftly at him, but he was smiling. 'Ah well, that's the way Fate works,' he continued gently. 'It looks as if I shall continue to be lonely until my holiday is over.'

'I'm not seeing Donato tonight,' I responded, feeling guilty. 'But he is taking me out tomorrow afternoon.'

'You're looking pale. Are you feeling

shocked?' Concern sounded in his voice and his expression showed anxiety.

'I'm all right now,' I asserted.

'Where has he taken your car?'

'I told you, to his father's garage.'

'Where is that?'

'I don't know.' I shook my head, smiling. 'You don't think he'd try and steal it, do you? He's left a much better car outside for my use.'

'I wouldn't dream of suggesting anything like that,' he said gravely. 'But one cannot be too careful.'

'I need a shower.' I moved to the stairs. 'It's been an afternoon I shan't forget in a hurry.'

'You've been very lucky,' observed the receptionist. 'Be very careful in future.'

I nodded and smiled, but thought her warning ominous as Paul accompanied me to my room.

5

As we reached my room, I paused and looked at Paul. There was eagerness in his eyes. 'Would you care to see the Trevi Fountain this evening?' he invited.

'I'd love to! I meant to visit it before my holiday was over. Thank you for asking me. It's the fountain where one must throw a coin into the water, isn't it?'

'That's the popular tradition, if you wish to return to Rome. I think it was started by the people who collect the coins!' He smiled, yet seemed ill at ease, and I wondered about that as we made arrangements for the evening.

Taking a refreshing shower, I told myself that Paul was perhaps jealous of Donato's advent into my life, and the fact that I was intent on seeing the Italian again. It pleased me to think that a comparative stranger could care, but then

I thought of the situation that existed here at the hotel, what with the receptionist and all, and when I was wrapped in my dressing gown I went to the window to check if the stocky Italian was outside. I saw nothing of him, and began to prepare for the evening, filled with a sense of relief.

A knock at the door startled me, and I went to answer, still in my dressing gown. The receptionist was outside, smiling and holding a large bouquet of red roses wrapped in cellophane and tied with a pink ribbon. 'For you,' she said needlessly, and I gasped and thanked her.

Closing the door, I looked at the card with the flowers and saw Donato's signature beneath a few words. The message read: 'To the only English rose I know!' I smiled dreamily and leaned against the door. That was a nice gesture, and so romantic. My heart thudded as I put the roses in a vase. Considering the forthcoming evening with Paul, I felt confused by the attentions of two men.

My solitude-loving soul could not find room for two apparent admirers, and between the pair of them it seemed that I would get little work done.

I wore a pale yellow dress, carried my white shoulder bag, and was waiting for Paul at seven o'clock. Promptly on the hour a firm knock at the door announced his arrival, and I felt a stir of eagerness as I went in reply. As soon as I opened the door I realised that it was a mistake. The room was filled with the heavy scent of the roses. Paul sniffed, and then looked past me and saw the vase.

'Hello,' he said, narrowing his eyes. 'Let me guess. They're from your new Latin admirer.'

'That's fairly obvious,' I responded, somewhat stung by the tone of his voice. 'You know I haven't met anyone else in Rome except you and Donato.'

'That's true.' His expression softened and he smiled. 'Certainly more romantic than your average Englishman, eh? I'm a bit niggled that I didn't think to send you flowers.'

We left the hotel, and I soon forgot my fears as Paul's personality impressed itself upon me. He was a quiet-natured type, not as flamboyant as Donato, but there was something about him that got through all the barriers. We walked down the Via del Tritone from the Piazza Barbarini and turned into the Via Poli, which led straight to most celebrated of Roman fountains. I had seen postcards of the Fontana di Trevi, watched a film about it, and had seen it in a documentary on television, but none had done full credit to the scene that awaited my wondering eyes.

Forming a backdrop to the fountain was a building in the style of a baroque triumphal arch, and in the centre niche stood an immense statue of Neptune in a conch-shaped chariot drawn by horses whose tossing heads were being held by tritons. The foaming water flowed into three superimposed basins before gushing into a larger pool. On either side of the centrepiece, miniature waterfalls splashed and gurgled from an artistic disarray of yellow rocks. The building was topped by figures representing the four seasons, and statues of Health and Abundance filled the lateral niches.

Paul was watching my face as I absorbed the scene. There were some fifty people around the fountain, mainly tourists, and cameras were clicking. The hot air seemed unduly fresh. Paul used my camera to take several snaps of me in various positions in front of the fountain, and I cast my coin into the blue water, closing my eyes as I made a wish to return some day to this most beautiful of all cities.

We sat on the parapet and talked, but I soon realised that Paul said very little about himself, and that fact jarred. Deep down, I was still suspicious of him, thinking that he was the unknown man who had wanted information about me before my arrival. Later, we walked back to the hotel, strolling in the fading sunlight, and I enjoyed the peacefulness and Paul's company. Yet there was something bothering me, and it wasn't until Paul asked, 'Why do you keep glancing back over your shoulder?' that I realised what it was.

'I have a feeling that we're being followed,' I replied without thought, and saw a frown appear between his blue eyes. I gulped, for the words opened up my mind and permitted fresh fears to filter through.

'That mysterious little Italian, I suppose,' he remarked. 'But you don't have to worry about him while you're in my company. I learned judo in my youth, and backed it up with karate. I have a black belt in judo.'

'That makes you a very tough customer,' I said slowly. 'You seem to have made good use of your spare time. You've learned languages and how to defend yourself. But you haven't said much about your past. Are you married?'

'No.' He smiled. 'I've led a very uneventful life; never done anything worth talking about. I live in London.'

'That's a very big city. Can't you be more precise?'

'Wimbledon. We'll exchange addresses, if you like. I live at home with my parents. My father owns a sheet-metal factory and my mother works as his secretary.'

'And you didn't go into your father's business?'

'I'm not very good with my hands, and sitting behind a desk every day doesn't appeal to me.' He glanced around, and then looked into my eyes. 'You've got me doing it now.' He smiled, his eyes gleaming. 'You haven't seen that mysterious Italian since the Spanish Steps, have you?'

'No. I've kept an eye open for him, but he hasn't revealed himself.'

'Then it might have been a coincidence. I shouldn't worry about him if I were you.'

'But you're not me, and I'm not skilled in the martial arts.'

'I could give you some lessons,' he observed.

I smiled. 'Thanks, but I'm not the type.'

'What would you do if you were

suddenly attacked?' His tone was serious, and I glanced at him. He looked tense, and nodded as I met his gaze. 'It happens every day,' he declared.

'Please change the subject, if you don't mind,' I told him, glancing over my shoulder again. Then I pulled myself up mentally. 'How about buying a woman a drink?' I suggested. 'It's very hot this evening.'

'Certainly. There's a café just along here.'

We sat at a table on the pavement outside, watching the traffic flowing noisily. I had a liqueur that tasted like Benedictine. I studied Paul's strong features as he glanced around, and I could tell that he was tense and on the lookout for any trouble. When his eyes flickered to me, I smiled. 'You have a habit of being on your guard,' I declared. 'I noticed it when we first met at the hotel.'

'Really?' He smiled and shrugged his powerful shoulders, his blond hair gleaming in the failing light of evening sunset.

'Yes, you're very alert.'

'It must be my judo training,' he replied. He smiled easily. 'What are you doing tomorrow morning? You're seeing your new Italian friend tomorrow afternoon and evening, aren't you?'

'Donato is taking me to the Villa Borghese in the afternoon. He's promised me a ride in a horse cab through the avenues, and in the evening we're going to a café owned by his friends.'

'That sounds interesting. May I see you in the morning? What are your plans?'

'I'm thinking of taking in the Colosseum and making plenty of notes. I think I'd better go alone, because I need to concentrate.'

'Very well. Perhaps we can get together again the day after tomorrow?'

'Certainly. I've enjoyed this evening. It's been very peaceful and restful. But I'm ready to work now, and I must make an effort to get something down on paper.'

'Shall we make our way back to the hotel now?' He rose and came around to my side to ease back my chair as I arose. I noticed that he glanced surreptitiously at his watch, and when we continued our stroll he seemed to be in just a little bit of a hurry.

When we reached the hotel, the shadows were quite dense in the courtyard. There was a lamp burning over the entrance, its brilliance causing the surrounding darkness to appear black and impenetrable. I saw Donato's Fiat in half-shadow, and felt my lips soften as I recalled that afternoon. Meeting Donato had been most pleasant after I had recovered from the shock of the accident, and the roses had been a crowning touch. But Paul made me feel guilty, for he was on holiday and had admitted to being lonely. We had got on very well, and if it had not been for all the mystery and menace I might have felt more strongly about him — but in my mind he was inextricably connected with the anonymous little Italian and the inscrutable receptionist.

As we entered the lobby, the eponymous lady looked up. She was always on duty, it seemed, no matter what time of day. 'Good evening,' she greeted us cheerfully in her faultless English. 'Have you enjoyed your evening?'

'It was lovely,' I replied. 'I hope it's true what they say about throwing a coin into the Trevi Fountain.'

'Ah, so that's where you've been.' She smiled and nodded. A glitter came into her eyes as she glanced at Paul and spoke rapidly in Italian, which of course I understood perfectly. 'Mr Russell, there was a telephone call from a colleague of yours. He needs to see you rather urgently at his home.'

Paul nodded, his face serious for a moment. Then he glanced at me and smiled.

'That sounded like quite a mouthful of a message,' I commented. 'I wish I could speak Italian.'

'There's nothing like speaking to the natives to perfect one's command of their language,' he said, 'and that's why

I've asked the receptionist to always speak to me in Italian. She merely said that there is no better sight in Roma than the Trevi Fountain, and she hopes we'll both return to the city in due course, and together. That's the romantic Italians for you. She's trying her hand at matchmaking!'

I smiled and nodded, but my face was a mask, and inside I felt stiff and cold. He had lied to me! I understood Italian as well as if not better than he, and knew exactly what the receptionist had said. I fought down the impulse to blurt out my knowledge. All my suspicions of him hardened, for I could see no reason why he should lie — but I meant to find out. If he was up to no good, then I wanted to know about it.

'I think it is time to call it a day,' I said, pushing my tumultuous thoughts into the background. 'I'm thoroughly exhausted.'

Paul nodded and grasped my arm as we ascended the stairs. We paused at my door, and I knew what was going to happen but could not move. He took me into his arms, holding me very gently, and kissed me lightly on the lips. For a few moments his blue eyes were closed, but I kept mine open, gazing at him, wondering why I was feeling so unresponsive. All through the evening I had been anticipating this moment, and wanting it to happen, but now I was feeling like ice inside. Then he opened his eyes and released me, stepping back.

'I'm sorry but I'm very tired,' I said, to explain my lack of response.

I felt sorry for him, yet could not overlook the situation surrounding us. He was involved in this mystery, and until I knew what it was all about I could not trust him.

'Well, goodnight,' he said in a neutral tone. 'You'd better lock your door tonight.'

'Don't worry; I locked it last night, and I shall lock it every night.'

He nodded and turned away. My heart softened a little. 'Goodnight, Paul,' I replied. 'Thank you for a very lovely evening. I really enjoyed it.'

He looked back as he went to his room and smiled. As I entered my room and locked the door, a host of strange and confusing emotions filled me. I liked Paul a great deal, but there was something about him that did not ring true.

* * *

The next morning I visited the Colosseum as planned, and spent a fruitful time browsing through that fabulous monument to the glory that was Rome. I bought a guide book, which would save me the trouble of making copious notes, and let my imagination run wild as I peered up at the crumbling stone edifice that had withstood the ravages of time. There were faint white clouds drifting overhead, and as I stood gazing up at the countless arches I felt as if the entire building was about to fall down around my ears.

This was a site where blood had been spilled in great quantities. Men had fought other men, and beasts, for the pleasure of those ancient Romans. Christians had been martyred here. Every stone was steeped in violence, and I shivered as the atmosphere seemed to grasp me by the throat.

I spent all morning at the Colosseum and was well satisfied as I went back to the hotel. I had finally made a start on the working part of my holiday and would not feel guilty when I met Donato later.

I didn't see Paul at lunch, and wondered if his business had kept him. Donato arrived punctually at the hotel, as he had said he would. I was wearing my best blue dress with the short sleeves. His expressive brown eyes gleamed when he saw me descending the stairs. He was standing in the lobby, talking casually with the receptionist, but paused and nodded emphatically at my appearance.

'You're as pretty as a picture!' he

declared, and, despite the trite greeting I was flattered. He came forward, took my hand and pressed it to his lips. I felt heat flush my cheeks, for the receptionist was standing stolidly behind her desk, watching me intently.

'Thank you for the roses,' I said. 'They're beautiful. Their scent filled my room.'

'They are a tribute to your beauty,' he replied. 'I am glad you liked them. Did you have a pleasant morning?'

'It was a productive one.' I smiled and he took my arm and led me to the door. 'I shan't feel guilty about enjoying myself this afternoon.'

I gave him the keys to the Fiat and he opened the passenger door for me. When he slid in behind the wheel I looked into his eyes. 'What's happening with my car?' I asked. 'Is it badly damaged?'

'It will need two rear wheels, but otherwise the damage is mainly superficial. It will need a re-spray and new rear lights, and when it is finished it will be better than before. I am not so fortunate. My car is more badly damaged, but that is as it should be.'

I smiled, for he was so suave and charming. I felt myself loosening up, and the tension that had gripped me slipped away as he pulled out from the hotel. He was a steady driver, and I took advantage of his attention to the traffic to study his profile, finding myself comparing him to Paul. A frown pulled at my forehead as I thought of the fair Englishman. More than ever, I was certain that he was somehow involved in whatever was developing at the hotel. His deliberate lie about what the receptionist had said did not fit his general character. I used characters all the time in my literary work and could sum up any person fairly accurately.

'A penny for them,' Donato cut in, and I jerked myself from my musing and smiled at him.

'I was just thinking how quickly the days seem to be passing, but it's always the same when one is enjoying oneself.'

'I'm glad to learn that you are happy, and I hope my presence has some small part in your frame of mind,' he replied.

'I admire your command of English,' I said, and he smiled, his face relaxing. 'I only wish I had learned some Italian before I came to Rome,' I added wistfully. 'It sounds such a warm, romantic language.'

'Perhaps I'll get the chance to teach you a few words before you return to England. Here we are now. I'll park the car and we'll take a ride in a horse cab.'

I looked around, having no idea where we were, but presently we found a parking space and I took my bag and camera with me when we left the car. We went to a spot where some horse-drawn cabs stood in a line in the shade of some trees. They were low, one-horse vehicles, open-topped, with the hood down at the back. Donato bargained vociferously with the driver for a ride around the Villa Borghese, and when a deal was agreed we stepped into the vehicle and settled down.

It was pleasant driving under the trees, with just the grating of the wheels and the clip-clop of the horse's hoofs marring the silence. Birds were singing in the branches overhead, and the sky was a perfect blue. I took in the scenery with a relaxed thankfulness, and Donato was most understanding. He said little, letting me enjoy the sights and giving me the occasional detail.

Other tourists seemed to have the same idea as us, for a number of *carroze* were plying their steady trade along the avenues. I permitted the scenery to wash over me. It was pleasant after the dense traffic in the city, and I wished the ride could go on indefinitely. Several times Donato called to the driver to halt, and I took snapshots of the scenes that caught my eye and imagination.

But suddenly the sense of peace was shattered, for amongst the teeming crowd, in an open space where several avenues converged, I spotted a face that I knew. It was the mysterious little man who had taken such an interest in my car in the hotel courtyard. I gasped aloud, causing Donato to glance quickly at me. He reached out and lightly touched my arm, alerted by my expression of shock.

'What is it, Gail? You look as if you've just seen a ghost.'

'Do you see that stocky little man over there, the one in the cream shirt and brown trousers?' I broke off, for an even greater shock struck me. The little Italian was walking around a group of tourists who were huddled over a street map, and standing just behind them was the tall, lithe figure of Paul Russell! 'Stop the cab,' I said, almost in a screech of panic, and Donato called instantly to the driver.

'What is wrong?' There was a tense note in Donato's voice. 'I see the little man. Is he someone you know? Who is the other man he is talking to?'

I held my breath as my hands clenched around my shoulder bag. I could not believe what I was seeing.

Paul and the little Italian were shaking hands, both smiling and talking. Paul was glancing around intently in his usual way. I hunched my shoulders, sank down in my seat and averted my face, afraid that Paul would spot me. But he knew I was coming here. I had told him so the previous evening.

Donato grasped my shoulder, and when I looked up at him I saw that his face was filled with a tense expression of curiosity and wonder. 'You are acting very strangely,' he said in marvellous understatement.

On an impulse I told him of the incidents that had occurred since my arrival, except for the conversation I had overheard in the hotel lobby between the receptionist and the unknown telephone caller. Donato listened intently, his face showing uncertainty as if he could not believe what he was hearing. When I lapsed into silence he shook his head.

'I'll go and confront them,' he said firmly. 'I'll soon find out what their business is.'

'No! That's the last thing you should do! Paul is a guest at my hotel, and I don't want him to discover that I suspect what he may be up to. He chased that man at the Spanish Steps, and now they're acting like old friends. What on earth is going on?'

'I can understand your caution, but I think this business should be checked out, and by the police,' Donato said firmly. He took my camera, adjusted the settings and snapped Paul and the Italian several times.

'What are you doing?' I demanded, gazing at him in surprise, and he patted my arm reassuringly and jumped out of the cab.

'Just sit still and stay low so they cannot see you. I'll be back in a moment.'

I watched as Donato hurried away to approach Paul and the Italian from a different direction. He used the camera several times, taking shots of various scenes, casually including Paul and the Italian in a close-up shot. A few minutes later he jumped into the cab beside me and ordered the driver to continue.

'Stay down!' Donato commanded. 'They have not looked in this direction, so I don't think they've seen you yet. It would be a pity to spoil things now.'

'Why did you take pictures of them?' I demanded, my brain reeling.

'My father is influential locally, and we have friends who are in the police. I think it would be a good idea to have a look at the pictures and perhaps make an investigation into the activities of those two. Don't worry! No harm will come to you. I will take a special interest in you now.'

'But what could possibly happen to me?' I asked foolishly.

'They are obviously up to no good, and the sooner we find out the better.'

I remained silent, not knowing what to make of this development. But the edge was gone from my peace of mind and there was no sense of pleasure left in me. I think, however, that my despondency stemmed from the fact that my instincts about Paul had been wrong. Individual details were beginning to add up to a disturbing total. Paul had deliberately lied to me on more than one occasion, and he certainly wasn't what he seemed. All I hoped was that Donato could get at the truth, and I felt extremely fortunate to have him on my side. He seemed to have the right connections, so I could only let him go ahead and handle matters. He seemed to be doing all right at the moment.

But what would happen next? How could I possibly face Paul again and maintain a façade of ignorance, when I possessed the knowledge of his deceit?

6

Donato certainly proved to be a man of action. He showed me around the Galleria Borghese, but my happy anticipation was shattered and I hardly took in any of the details I might need. I kept looking around nervously instead of studying the exhibits; and after Donato had spoken to me several times without my hearing him, he reached out and took hold of my hands.

'I can see that we are wasting our time,' he observed. 'Your mind is elsewhere at the moment, and these treasures deserve your undivided attention.'

'I'm sorry, Donato, but I'm not thinking straight.'

'You are not to blame. It is my fault. I should take your camera to the police immediately. They will soon check out those two men, and when your mind is put at rest you'll be able to enjoy yourself once more.'

'Perhaps you're right,' I said doubtfully, glancing around somewhat enviously at the other tourists filing through the galleries. 'I won't rest until I know what this is all about.'

'I had better take your camera to the police now. It will spoil our day, I'm afraid. But it will be better to lose one day now than ruin the rest of your holiday later.'

'I don't know what I've walked into here.' Anger tinged my voice. 'I certainly want to find out. Shall we go to the police now?'

'I don't think you should accompany me.' Donato's voice was firm, his gaze steady. 'How shall I put this?' He paused and glanced around. 'Just look at these other people. How do we know that one of these is not connected with the other two? There might be someone watching you, and they could stand at your elbow without you being aware of their real intentions.'

I gulped and nodded, scarcely able to

prevent myself from looking around like a frightened rabbit. 'If I accompany you to the police station, then he or she may follow us and realise that I suspect something. That's good thinking, Donato. I don't know what I'd do without your help.'

'I have my wits about me because I live in Rome,' he replied. 'I have helped our police on several occasions. It is a public duty that I take seriously.'

'So what are you going to do now?'

'Take you back to the hotel and leave you there. I doubt if I shall be followed — I am not of interest — but I shall take precautions even so. I am sorry to spoil your day like this, but I think it is the right thing to do.'

'I agree with you wholeheartedly. The uncertainty about this is beginning to have an effect on my nerves. I'll be having nightmares next.'

'Then we shall leave now.'

He seemed anxious as he took my arm, and some of his concern communicated itself to me. I glanced around warily as we departed, and Donato shook my arm gently.

'Act normally,' he advised me. 'Smile. Show that you are in a carefree mood. If you look so worried, a casual passer-by may just think we are married, but those two men will suspect that you are worried about them.'

I nodded and smiled, but his words merely added to my uneasiness. We returned to the car and drove back to the hotel. Donato did not enter the hotel but parked at its entrance.

'Complain of a headache,' he suggested.

'When shall I see you again?'

'I'll get in touch with you as soon as I have any news. But it could be some time, perhaps not until tomorrow. If you go out alone before I contact you, make sure you do not visit any lonely places.'

'Now you're frightening me,' I told him, suppressing a shiver. 'Supposing Paul comes back to the hotel and asks me to go out with him?'

'Do not make him suspect that you are suspicious of him, and don't let yourself be deceived into a position of jeopardy.'

'You have a quaint way of putting it into words, but I get your point.' I started to get out of the car but he grasped my arm, and when I turned to him he held out his hand.

'I must have your camera.'

'Of course! I'll give you the memory card. I have another with me so that I can keep using my camera if I need to.' I opened the camera and removed the memory card, which he took from me and dropped into his pocket.

'I'll get it back to you so you still have your other shots,' he promised.

'Thank you. Is there any chance of seeing you this evening? I'm worried by all this. I want to know what's going on.'

'So do I!' His expression was grim. 'I won't telephone you here because the receptionist might listen in on the call, but rest assured that I will come and see you as soon as I can.'

'You really think that Paul and his little friend are up to no good?'

'What else can it be?' He shook his head. 'I don't like it at all, and I'm not saying this to frighten you. I merely want you to face up to the facts.'

'I shall certainly be careful.' For a moment I looked into his handsome face and studied his gleaming eyes. He seemed so serious that the unreality of the situation passed away from my thoughts and I felt the extreme gravity of what might be hanging over me. I almost blurted out that I knew much more than I had told him, but again something prevented me from informing him of the telephone conversation I had overheard. I did not want him to know that I had lied to him about my understanding of his language.

Alighting from the car, I entered the courtyard and walked into the hotel. The receptionist was behind the deck — I should have been surprised if she was not — and her dark eyes flickered as she glanced up at me. I almost succumbed to the temptation to confront her, but realised that I had to give Donato time to get to the police. If the law could identify the stocky Italian, then part of the mystery might be explained. I already suspected that he was a small-time crook and imagined that he and Paul were working together in some unlawful business that somehow would involve me.

'You are back early, Miss Bennett,' the receptionist said.

'I have a headache, and my stomach feels slightly upset,' I replied.

'Ah!' She nodded. 'The change of water and the food can have that effect on sensitive stomachs. And we do try so hard to make your meals almost what you are accustomed to.'

'I'm not blaming the hotel. The food here is marvellous. I think I'm just trying to do too much! I ought to spend my first week quietly sight-seeing, then working during the second week. But I'm a glutton for work.'

I turned away from the desk and walked to the stairs, and at that moment a shadow darkened the doorway and I glanced around to see Paul entering the hotel. My heart seemed to jump up into my throat as I gazed at him. He merely smiled casually and came over to me. I took a deep breath and smiled back.

'You didn't stay out long,' he commented.

'She has another headache,' the receptionist said, and again I gained the impression that she was in league with Paul.

'I'm sorry to hear that. I noticed the Fiat is not outside. Has your friend taken it back?'

'He's bringing it back later,' I said easily.

'I hope your headache will ease. Do you have any aspirin?'

'I do have some, but I won't take any. I'll lie down for a spell and I'm sure it will go.'

'I'll look in on you later to see how you are,' he promised. 'I remember I was like that in my first week — it's the change of routine, the food, and the water.'

I nodded and ascended the stairs. A sigh of relief escaped me when I entered my room. I cut my sigh short and hurried to the window, looked around, and my relief grew when I failed to see the stocky Italian. All the talk of a headache had set my temples throbbing for real, and I thought I would be a nervous wreck by the end of my holiday.

Paul remained in my thoughts. I had liked him from the moment we'd met, and my instincts were not usually wrong. But he had not told me anything about his background beyond the fact that he was an insurance agent, which I did not believe for a minute. His manner and attitude were all wrong for his type. I had learned early through my journalistic training that one could not rely on appearances, but there was something about him that seemed artificial. What could his business really be? He had been in Rome for two weeks. How could he have known I was arriving? I was perplexed. He was very friendly with the receptionist. But why would he have telephoned the hotel just after my arrival when he was staying under the same roof as me, and could easily have just talked to the receptionist face to face?

But it could have been the stocky Italian who had inquired about my arrival, the mystery man Paul had supposedly chased at the Spanish Steps and yet knew well enough to shake hands with and chat to in a friendly fashion at the Villa Borghese.

I was frustrated and gave up thinking about it. Instead, I took out my notebook and forced myself to settle down to some work. But, human nature being what it is, trying to push the problems into the background only succeeded in making them more present in my mind. I simply could not accept that Paul was up to no good.

I put aside my work and again tried

to puzzle out what might be going on. My thoughts veered from one side of the mystery to the other and went around in circles as well. Why had the stocky Italian followed me? That question brought me to another, more interesting thought — if he and Paul could follow me, then why couldn't I do the same? If I could learn something of their activities, then I might be better placed to work out the real reason behind them.

I left the room and went downstairs. A glance at the clock on the wall informed me that I had been in my room for just over an hour. The receptionist looked intently at me, her expression showing concern, and I smiled.

'I feel better already,' I told her.

'But you are not going out again so soon, are you?'

'No, it's too late to do anything more this afternoon. I think I'll sit in the shade on the terrace until it's time for tea.'

'I'll tell Mr Russell where you are if

he comes down. He's most concerned about you.'

'That's kind of him.' I walked out to the small terrace, where three small tables were set overlooking the courtyard. Determination was beginning to build in my mind. I was not going to sit around idly and let some evil plot unfold around me. I wanted to know what was going on, and I meant to find out.

Barely ten minutes passed before the cream Fiat came swinging into the courtyard, and I almost sprang to my feet in relief. Donato halted the car and I ran down the steps to greet him. He remained in the vehicle and motioned for me to join him. A chill stabbed through me as I slid into the front passenger seat, for Donato's features were grim and I was certain he had bad news.

'I went to the police department where my friends are. I explained the situation, and when I described that small Italian man they showed me some pictures. Within ten minutes I had spotted him.'

'He has a criminal record?'

'He certainly has! His name is Alfredo Rinaldi and he's a jewel thief, although he is not averse to dabbling in anything criminal.'

'Why should he be interested in me? I don't have any jewels.' I fell silent, remembering that my room had been searched. Questions teemed in my mind, but I could find no answers. I drew a deep breath. 'And what about Paul Russell?'

'Our police have nothing on him, but they are checking with Interpol.'

'I was thinking of trying to follow him to find out what his business is.'

'We shall soon know. My friends have asked me to tell you to be very careful and act as if you are completely unaware of whatever is going on. Don't be worried if you get the feeling that you are being watched, because detectives are being put on the case and will keep an eye on you, although they do not want to come too close for fear of alerting Rinaldi. They suggest that you make an effort to be in Russell's company as much as possible and try to learn what you can about him without arousing his suspicions. You can report to me, and I will pass on anything you learn. That way the police can remain at arm's length and not alarm these men with any undue activity.'

'That will be easy to accomplish,' I said eagerly. 'I decided this afternoon to try something of that nature because I was curious. Paul keeps asking me to go out with him, but I don't think I shall learn anything from him. He's very close-mouthed. He'll make certain that I don't set eyes on Rinaldi again, because I know him by sight.'

'It's not so much that. The police would like you to talk to Russell, and more importantly to listen to him. He might let something slip that could give a clue to his intentions.'

I could feel my journalist's mind working overtime and fought down the eagerness that filled me. But underneath the eagerness there was disappointment, for I knew that I liked Paul. I tried to blot out my personal feelings and nodded. 'I'll do what I can,' I said.

Donato nodded. 'Good. I'll inform the police. I'd better drop out of your life for a few days, but I'll leave the car for you.'

'Is there somewhere I can contact you in case I should learn something important?'

'I think that would be unwise at this time. There's no telling if they are having me watched now that I have become friendly with you. Until we discover what it is they are up to, I think we should not take any risks. And you must be very careful, Gail. This could be dangerous.'

'They won't get suspicious of me.' I sounded confident. 'I'm just an ordinary woman on holiday. Now what about my car, Donato?'

'It will be repaired in about a week.' He smiled. 'You will come out of this much better off than before. The garage will do a very good job. You have two new wheels on the back, and I'll put two new tyres on the front to make them the same all round.'

'That's very good of you.' I smiled. 'You're a life saver, Donato.'

'It's kind of you to say so. Now, I'd better go. Keep the car, and I'll be in touch with you later. Spend as much time as you can in Russell's company, and even if you don't learn anything, your presence may delay anything he has in mind — at least until the police can find out something about him.'

He smiled and alighted from the car. I got out and he locked up, handed the keys to me and departed quickly. I watched him go, my mind still staggered by the information he had imparted.

'Hello there!' Paul called from the doorway of the hotel. I turned to face him. He was smiling, tanned and confident. 'How are you feeling? I tapped on your door and didn't get a reply. The receptionist told me you were out here. Has your headache gone?'

'Yes, thanks. I'm fine now.'

'Why don't you forget about working for a few days? You're trying to do too much, too soon.'

'I've already decided that's my trouble, and I going to do nothing but sight-seeing for the next few days. I've got all next week to gather facts and make notes.'

'And your Italian friend? Are you going to see him? Or can I hope to share your company?'

'He's going away for several days on business, so I shall be alone.'

'Good.' He made no secret of his pleasure at the news, and I wondered what possible interest he could have in me. If he were a criminal then I couldn't help him at all, and certainly wouldn't willingly do anything to further whatever plans he was hatching.

'Let me work out a few tours for the next day or so that won't be too strenuous,' he added.

'Fine. I should like to see St Peter's

and some of the other major sights. Perhaps you wouldn't mind escorting me around?'

'It will be my pleasure.' He paused, his eyes twinkling as he smiled. 'By the way, you haven't seen that little Italian around again, have you?'

I fought to keep my face expressionless and shook my head. 'No, I haven't seen him. Perhaps the fact that you're with me has scared him off.'

'Well, I'd forget about him if I were you. There are some Italians who make a living by preying on unattached females, especially tourists. If they see competition of any weight and build, they usually disappear.'

'Thank goodness for that! He looked like a nasty little man, anyway. I wouldn't like to meet him alone and in the dark.'

'There's no chance of that with me around,' Paul said, and I couldn't help wondering how safe I would actually be with him.

7

We went to tea, and when Paul asked me to go out with him that evening I fought down an impulse to refuse. I would learn nothing about him unless I associated with him, and a strange sense of unreality entered my mind as we set out in the Fiat in the early evening. The sun was still shining, and Paul was driving the car, so I gave my full attention to looking at the sights. It felt strange, being in his company and liking him, despite the knowledge that he was most probably a criminal and potentially planning to involve me in some nefarious business.

'Where are we going?' I asked.

'When I showed you the Aventine Hill, I pointed across the Tiber and you saw the Janiculum Hill, where I said there's a statue of Garibaldi. The best time of day to see the finest view in

Rome is early evening as the sun is setting. The masses of rooftops are gilded, and the Alban Hills in the background are purple. That's where we're going. It's a sight you'll never forget.'

'You're quite poetic,' I said, smiling. But underneath my apparent casualness there was a sweltering tension, and I hoped my manner and expression would not betray me. It was quite a strain to try and appear outwardly normal while I was filled with the darkest suspicions.

'When you've been in Rome a few more days you'll begin to understand why so many of our poets came here in the last century,' he said.

We left the car in a convenient space and walked up the Via Garibaldi, going straight to the immense monument to the eponymous man, who had organised the defence of the Republic of Rome. I had done some pre-reading on him, and it was interesting to study the mounted figure atop its plinth that gazed down with sightless stone eyes. The bas-relief of the hero's deeds commemorated there was imposing, and I felt a sense of awe as I peered around, my romantic mind conjuring up the events of the past.

The view from here was beautiful, and I could see other monuments around, but I was not going to view them all. This was one of the hills on which Rome had been built, and I was already feeling leg-weary. Paul pointed out a walk along a ridge and suggested we take it. 'There's a tree-lined square with a fountain along there,' he said.

'I'm sure it's lovely, but it's taking me longer to get acclimatised than I imagined it would, and I don't want to overdo it. Am I being a bore?'

'Certainly not!' Paul shook his head and glanced at me quickly, as if trying to catch me out or surprise me. It was a most disconcerting habit he had, and I was hard put to remain expressionless.

'Tell me something about yourself,' I said. 'What are your likes and dislikes? What do you find most interesting in

Rome? What brought you here in the first place?'

'The same reason that has brought millions of tourists through the centuries.' There was a smooth tone in his voice, but he looked around again alertly. 'I thought I had told you all about myself,' he added.

'I don't think so. You know a great deal about me, but I don't even know your London address.' I paused. 'What insurance company do you work for? You haven't tried to sell me any insurance. You haven't even asked me if I'm covered for this holiday.'

'I'm not the kind of man who goes around door to door selling personal insurance and collecting premiums,' he responded, smiling quaintly, his pale blue eyes gleaming in the setting sunlight. 'For every man in the field actually handling the business, there are many others who back them up. I have a very humdrum sort of job. It's all figures — computer sheets, that sort of thing.'

'My apologies,' I replied, smiling. 'So you're really a clerk with an insurance company.'

'That's right. Did I mislead you in any way? I hope I didn't give you the impression that I was someone of importance in my little area of activity.'

He sounded so pleasant and ordinary that I found it difficult to concentrate on the instructions Donato had given me. But there was no doubt that Paul was associating with a known criminal, and it couldn't have been someone he had met while on holiday. The facts contradicted themselves. He had chased the man at the Spanish Steps, conveniently unable to catch him in the crowd, and the next day was shaking hands with him at the Villa Borghese.

I gazed out across the rooftops and watched the skyline, where purple hills stood out stark and remote, and realised that no matter what questions I asked Paul I would get no real information from him. He had a manner, a glibness about him that shrugged off questions like raindrops. He could turn a question adroitly, and I wondered if it was all a part of his real self — if the man I thought I knew was just a projection he wished me to accept.

What was he like deep inside? Did he kick dogs out of his path? Was he unkind to children? I could not tell merely by looking at him; and when I realised that my gaze had wandered from the view to pinpoint his face and that he was watching me while I gaped at him, I came to the conclusion that I had better forget about my clumsy attempts at investigation and inform Donato at the first opportunity that the police would have to do their own dirty work.

'You've got something on your mind, Gail,' Paul said abruptly. 'What's troubling you?'

It was the first time he had used my name so casually, and I jerked at the sound of it. 'I've always got something on my mind,' I returned, telling myself that two could play at his game. 'I never stop working, you know. That's the way it is for a writer. All impressions, scenes and scraps of conversation must be captured and stored away for future use. I told you I'm not good company, and this is a working holiday for me.'

He nodded slowly, apparently satisfied with my explanation. 'I suppose I am really a nuisance to you. You did tell me at the outset that you needed to be alone.'

'Now you're making me sound like Greta Garbo.' I chuckled lightly.

'If you're tired of walking, we could round off the evening with a drive,' he suggested.

'Anything to keep the weight off my feet.'

We descended the hill and returned to the car. I was finding it difficult to think of Paul as a criminal and could only wonder at the lapse of my instincts. I couldn't help but be curious about what type of crime he specialised in. Watching him covertly as he drove me around Rome in the gathering shadows, I realised that he was a man of many secrets. His manner suggested it, and he had that habit of glancing around unexpectedly, as if half-expecting a policeman to lay a hand on his collar.

But I enjoyed myself despite the doubts in my mind; and whatever else he might have been, Paul Russell was certainly good company. He named the streets through which we drove, and I looked at the lights and signs and took in the atmosphere of Rome at night.

'We must have a formal evening out,' he observed later, as we were returning to the hotel. 'There are some very good night clubs.' He glanced sideways at me. 'Do you like that sort of thing, or are you more for the cinema, or perhaps the theatre or opera?'

'I have a wide range of interests. With my work, I have to be interested in everything.'

'So you're easy to please!'

We were silent then, for some considerable time. I was considering the situation with a strange detachment, as if I did not really believe the facts. I felt comfortable in Paul's company despite what I knew about him, and that worried me. What would I do if I actually discovered that he was a criminal engaged in some nefarious project? Could I tell Donato, who would pass on the information to the police? I gazed from the car as we drove through a long, wide square where coloured lights turned cascading fountains into beautiful fantasies of fairyland proportions.

I sighed heavily, for I was living a fantasy. But when I thought of how much work I could have done had I not met Paul, and how much it had cost me to come to Rome — merely to become involved in a mystery that nagged at my peace of mind, I knew I should be angry. The surprising thing was, I felt no animosity at all.

When we pulled into the courtyard of the hotel, Paul parked the Fiat at the far end, in the deepest shadows. 'What about meeting up tomorrow?' he asked as I opened my door and the interior light came on.

I looked into his strong face and sought an excuse, but could not think of one. I sighed and shrugged slightly. 'I ought to settle down to some work,' I hedged. 'Let's leave it until tomorrow morning, shall we?'

'Certainly.' He alighted from the car and came around to my side, but I was out of the car and slamming the door before he could reach me. As he locked the door I walked to the entrance of the hotel, my eyes dazzled by the light issuing from the windows. He reached me as I ascended the steps, holding out the car keys. 'Thanks for a pleasant evening,' he said.

'Thank you,' I countered. 'I thoroughly enjoyed it.'

He was smiling easily, confident and self-assured, and I wondered what his expression would be if I suddenly blurted out all that I knew, and what Donato was planning. I suppressed a sigh and we entered the hotel.

The receptionist was at her desk, and she looked up from the book she was reading, a smile appearing on her lips. She nodded, lifting a hand. 'I hope you enjoyed your evening,' she said.

'It was most pleasant,' I replied, feeling a flatness beginning to invade my mind.

Paul began to explain where we had been and what we had seen, but she cut in quickly, speaking Italian so fast that I almost failed to catch what she said. But I did get the gist of it. There was a man in Paul's room waiting to talk to him. I maintained a blank expression as Paul threw one of his quick glances at me and turned to the stairs, calling a pleasant goodnight to the receptionist. My mind reeled with speculation as I ascended the stairs, and when we reached my door Paul seemed impatient to get away. He did not attempt to kiss me.

'I'll see you at breakfast then,' he said. 'Goodnight, Gail.'

'Goodnight,' I responded, my voice perfectly controlled as I smiled at him and let myself into my room. I closed the door firmly and shot the bolt, aware without glancing around that he was waiting to check that I was safely locked in. But as soon as I was out of his sight, my composure dissolved and I leaned against the door, feeling the strain of having maintained a casual manner all evening.

But there was the man waiting in Paul's room! That intrigued me. I had to discover who it was, or at least get a description of him, even if I could not overhear what they had to talk about. I did not switch on my light but crossed the gloomy room to the window, wishing there was a balcony to enable me to get outside Paul's window. There wasn't, of course!

For a few moments I was non-plussed, but my curiosity was aroused and I went back to the door and unbolted it, opening it a fraction and carefully holding it ajar. I stood in the darkness and peered out at the corridor with one eye applied to the half-inch crack. I did not know how long I should have to wait, but I was going to get a good look at Paul's visitor.

Minutes passed, and I kept blinking. My room was in darkness and the corridor was gloomy. I placed the toe of my right shoe against the bottom of the door to prevent it from opening any wider and fought down my impatience, telling myself that if I managed to solve the mystery there might be a good story in it for me.

Soon I heard a door opening and closing along the corridor. I tensed as I heard footsteps approaching. I moistened my lips and held my breath when two figures passed my door. One was Paul, who glanced at my door in passing, and for a frightening moment I imagined he would notice my door was not completely closed and might even be able to glimpse me. Then I looked at his companion, and was shocked rigid to recognise the stocky Italian, Rinaldo. This was my closest look at him. He was well into his forties, stocky and powerful: a small-time crook that was obviously more than a mere acquaintance of Paul's.

They went along the corridor and descended the stairs, and I opened my door quickly, looking out at them as they vanished from my sight. Where were they going? Excitement shot through me. Somehow, I had to follow them. Donato and his police friends would certainly want to know of any developments. I tightened my grip on the car keys, which were still in my hand, and left the room, closing the door quietly. But how could I get out of the lobby without being seen by the ever-present receptionist? I moved in the opposite direction, for there was a flight of stairs at the rear of the building: a fire escape. I descended, emerging into the courtyard from the street side of the hotel.

Paul and Rinaldi were leaving the courtyard, and I watched them cross to a car parked on the far side of the road. I darted through the shadows, gained the courtyard, and jumped into the Fiat. I did not switch on the lights as I backed out and headed for the street. When Rinaldi's car pulled away, I took a good look at it in order to be able to recognise it; then I switched on my lights and drove into the street to follow it.

There had to be something important happening for Rinaldi to come to the hotel and Paul to leave with him immediately, and I could hardly contain my excitement as I followed them carefully. Rinaldi's car was a red Fiat, and I made a mental note of its number for future reference. He did not drive fast; I supposed he did not want to attract attention to himself. Once I almost lost them, and followed nervously, afraid they would spot me, for Paul knew the car I was driving. But other cars kept cutting in between us, and I stayed back, watching their tail-lights turning left and right as they moved out of the centre of the city.

Then they reached a quieter area where there was not so much traffic, and I had to be even more careful. It seemed to be an industrial estate that we were passing through, and when Rinaldi braked and began to slow I pulled to the kerb and switched off my lights. Rinaldi turned a corner slowly, and I dared not follow in case they stopped suddenly. I took a chance and left the Fiat, hurrying along to the corner, and was relieved to see their car parked a dozen yards away, its lights switched off.

Was I about to solve a part of the mystery? Were they about to commit a crime? I swallowed nervously as anticipation gripped me. Paul and Rinaldi alighted from the car and moved into the shadows of a large building that towered blackly against the night sky.

I stayed at the corner, just able to distinguish their figures. Paul was the easier of the two to see, and he was standing to one side while Rinaldi bent at a door. I assumed he was doing something to the lock, for it took him several minutes to open a small door set in a much larger sliding door. They entered the building and the door closed.

I waited tensely, looking for lights to be switched on, but there was nothing to relieve the gloom, and a sense of anticlimax gripped me. I moved forward, against my better judgement; I needed some idea of what was going on. I passed their car and reached the building they had entered. There was a small window beside the door. Its glass was frosted and I could not see through it, but I caught the glimmer of a moving light inside the building and guessed they were using a torch.

My heart thudded as I went to the door and tried the handle. It was locked on the inside. They were not taking any chances. But I was, and was only too aware of the fact. They might emerge any moment, without warning, and I would not be able to explain my presence if they confronted me. I turned and hurried back to the corner, and had hardly cleared it, pausing to glance back at the building, when I heard a door being opened. Paul and Rinaldi reappeared, the latter pausing to relock the door. I turned and ran back to the Fiat, and it came to me suddenly that I had to get back to the hotel before Paul did because he would certainly notice if the Fiat was missing.

I drove away quickly, turned out of the street, and set about finding my way back to the hotel. I soon discovered that on the way out I had paid far more attention to keeping Rinaldi's car in sight than to noting my surroundings, but I spotted landmarks that helped, and soon found familiar streets. Twenty minutes later I drove into the courtyard of the hotel, alighted quickly, and locked the car door with a trembling hand.

As I turned away from the car, a hand snaked over my right shoulder from behind and clamped over my mouth. I was too startled to cry out as I was lifted bodily and pulled back into denser shadows. My shock was overwhelming. My tongue seemed to stick to the roof of my mouth in terror. Then a harsh whisper cut through my mental fog of shock.

'It's all right. It's Donato. Be very quiet.'

I gasped in relief but was shaking violently as he released me. My legs seemed to have turned to jelly. I staggered, and had to lean against Donato for support.

'Look!' he commanded in a harsh tone. I blinked, trying to focus my gaze. I saw Paul running lightly up the steps to the hotel entrance, his figure showing clearly for a brief moment under the lamp over the doorway. Then he disappeared inside, and a delayed reaction began to claw through me, leaving me weak and trembling.

'You almost scared the life out of me, Donato!' I gasped, turning to face him. 'What are you doing here?'

'I came to talk to you, but saw the car was gone. I waited for you to return. But you switched off the lights as you came into the courtyard as if you didn't want anyone to see you. Then Paul Russell got out of a car on the other side of the street opposite the entrance, and I just put two and two together.'

'And you came up with a very good four!' I sighed heavily, still feeling weak at the knees. 'I just made it back before them.'

'Tell me about it,' he said curtly.

I explained everything while he listened in silence. It all seemed so unnatural — standing in the shadows with his arms around me; telling him about Paul, whom I liked very much; and explaining that I thought Paul and Rinaldi had broken into the building to which I had followed them. But the facts were incontrovertible, and my heart felt heavy as I lapsed into silence.

Donato sighed. His face was just a pale blur in the light coming from the windows of the hotel. 'I don't like you running risks. I tremble to think of what might have happened to you if they had discovered what you were doing. I'll report this to the police.

You'll be interested to know that they have learned something about Paul Russell from Interpol. Russell has a criminal record. He specialises in stealing jewels. And the fact that Rinaldi is a known jewel thief indicates that the two of them have got together to carry out a big theft in Rome.'

'They're certainly working together, if what I saw tonight is anything to go by,' I replied, shaking my head. 'I don't know where it was they went tonight. It looked like a business area. Could it be that they are after industrial diamonds, or something of that nature?'

'I doubt it. From what the police told me, I think those two are interested only in valuable pieces of jewellery. But you could be right. I'll tell the police what you say.'

'And what about me? I don't think I can go on like this for much longer. The strain is too great. Paul Russell has such shrewd eyes, and I'm afraid my expression may give me away. I'm not accustomed to telling lies, and it might show.'

'I understand how you feel, Gail, but you are helping the police. You are much closer to Paul Russell than anyone in the city, and if you can learn anything at all about Russell's contacts the police would be very grateful. If they step in now, before they have enough evidence, the whole case may fall to pieces.'

'I understand that, but I don't see how I can be of much help. Paul isn't going to let me meet any of his friends.'

'He wasn't too careful this afternoon at the Villa Borghese.'

'That's true. He knew I was going there with you, and yet he showed up there to meet Rinaldi, whom I know by sight.' I bit my lip in exasperation, for although I liked Paul a lot despite what I knew about him, I did not care for anyone trying to make a fool out of me, and Paul was doing exactly that. 'All right, I'll see him tomorrow and try to get something from him. But you'd better get the police to check that area where I was this evening.' I gave him some directions. 'If they discover that a building was entered tonight then they'll know who the culprits are.'

'You've done extremely well.' Donato tightened his arms about me, and when he kissed me his lips were soft and gentle. 'I'm so sorry to involve you like this, but those two criminals are so very clever they would sense a police presence. It is very fortunate that you are in a position to help; and being a journalist, you could get a very worthwhile story for the newspapers.'

'Would the police let me have full details if I'm successful in getting some information from Paul?'

'I'll talk to them about it, but I am certain they will want to show their appreciation for your efforts. The story will be yours for the asking.'

I suppressed a sigh, for I was still keyed up by my experience, and there was a throbbing at my temples that seemed to presage a headache.

'I'd better go in now,' I said slowly. 'When shall I see you again, Donato? I asked you to let me have a telephone number or an address where I could contact you if I should need you quickly, but you haven't given me any details.'

'It slipped my mind. I'll give you my home telephone number.' He produced a pen and a letter from an inside pocket, tore the back off the envelope, and scribbled on it. 'Keep this in your handbag,' he said, handing the scrap of paper to me, 'and only use the number if it is a matter of urgency. If I don't happen to be there when you call then leave a message for me to call you here at the hotel. I will make a point of checking for any calls from you.'

I nodded, feeling extremely tired. I might be a good journalist with a flair for writing fiction, but I certainly wasn't cut out for this cloak-and-dagger stuff.

'Goodnight, Donato,' I said. 'This is one holiday I am not going to forget in a hurry.'

'If it works out as it should, I'll see to it that you have good cause not to forget it,' he replied, squeezing my hands.

His face was a pale oval in the gloom,

but I could remember it as I had seen it that afternoon. He was such a handsome man. Yet I could not raise any real enthusiasm for him, because Paul attracted me and I was vividly aware of it. Both Paul and Donato had kissed me, and although Donato was charming and debonair while Paul was quiet and serious, it seemed that Paul had aroused a greater response in me, and I could only marvel at the fact as I slipped through the shadows to the back stairs.

What would my mother say if she knew what I was doing? No matter how this turned out, I knew I would never have the nerve to tell her, for she would certainly make a big fuss about my way of life. There had to be a limit to what a woman could become involved in, and if I hadn't reached that dangerous boundary yet, I was almost certainly walking a tightrope over it.

8

The next morning when I awoke, I lay thinking sleepily about the situation that seemed to have enveloped me. Paul was a criminal. But I liked him! My lips tingled at the memory of his kiss, while Donato's had left no physical or mental impression on me. Donato was a pleasant man and a good friend, but I knew instinctively that he could never become anything more than that. So what was I going to do? If I gathered proof about Paul's criminal activities, would I have the strength to betray him? Or could I warn him that the local police were aware of his activities in Rome?

As I showered and dressed, I turned over the facts in my mind and came to the conclusion that I could not warn Paul. I would be breaking the law and might even make myself an accessory after the fact, as I was aware that he was acting illegally, and my warning would enable him to escape the consequences. I felt bound by my own sense of justice to help the police, but I couldn't pretend to like it.

Paul knocked at the door as I was putting the finishing touches to my make-up, and I opened it. He was fresh-looking, smelling of aftershave, and had no doubt slept soundly without any pang of conscience. I drew a deep breath and tried to subdue the emotions that threatened to break free of my control.

'Hello,' he greeted me, smiling. 'How are you feeling this morning? Did you sleep well?'

'I'm fine, thank you. Never slept better!' I hoped my face did not belie my words.

'Are you ready for breakfast?'

'I certainly am!' It took an effort to pack enthusiasm into my tone, but I managed it, and smiled as I left the room.

We went down to the dining room,

and during breakfast I felt the urge to warn him of what I knew. But there were still some facets of the mystery that I did not understand. Where did I fit into all this? Why had someone wanted to know about me? If they were going to use me, which was the only explanation for what had happened, then how were they going to do it?

I knew I had to have some answers to my questions, if only for my own peace of mind, and I strengthened my determination to follow Donato's instructions. From this moment Paul would not be able to go anywhere without having me along. He had followed me to the Spanish Steps, and two could play at that game.

I could not help wondering if the police had a report this morning of a robbery in the area where I had followed Paul and Rinaldi the previous evening. I had to curb my impatience; Donato would tell me in due course. But the waiting was the worst part of it.

'A penny for them,' said Paul, and I

jerked myself from my thoughts with a nervous start.

'Oh, I'm writing an article in my mind,' I replied without hesitation. 'It's how I work. That's one of the reasons I don't have a boyfriend. He wouldn't be able to bear the long silences when I slip away to that little ivory tower in my mind.'

'Escapism!' he retorted. 'That's what it is, a form of escapism. You don't like the world you live in so you invent your own utopia.'

'Quite possibly. I am God to my characters. I hold the power of life and death over them. I can twist any situation to my own advantage.'

'I hadn't looked at it like that, but you're right, of course, and I don't know how you can do it.'

There was admiration in his expression, and for a moment he fooled me completely with his genuine manner. Then I told myself that he was being friendly and pleasant because he wanted to use me in some unknown way, and I vowed that whatever happened, I should not be deceived.

'What are your plans for today?' he asked, forcing me to forget my thoughts and concentrate on more mundane things.

'I haven't decided yet. I thought it might be time to visit St Peter's. It is high on my list.'

'May I escort you in case that stocky little Italian is sneaking around in the background?'

'Yes, I'd like that,' I said immediately, and a cold pang stabbed through me because he was lying through his teeth and smiling while he did it.

'Shall we use the Fiat, or take a bus?' he asked me. 'I know my way around Rome pretty well, and it would be better not to have the car. Then we won't have the worry of parking it.'

'You've done well in your two weeks here,' I said. 'I don't think I should be able to find my way around in two months.'

'I'm used to travelling. It's just a

knack for memorising routes and places.'

'I've done a fair amount of travelling myself,' I replied. 'But I think we had better travel by bus. It will be simpler.'

'If you've finished breakfast then I suggest we make an early start. It will take the whole day to see everything I have in mind, and even then we'll have to miss out a good deal.'

'Fine.' I nodded and arose from the table. 'I'll get my camera and my bag and then I'll be ready.'

'I'll wait for you in the lobby.' He clasped my elbow as we left the dining room, and I felt something akin to an electric shock pass through me. He was the most disconcerting man, and I tried hard to keep my emotions under control as I went back up to my room, telling myself it would not do to fall in love with him.

When I returned to the lobby Paul was using the telephone, and the receptionist eyed me gravely. I stood casually by the desk, listening to every word

Paul said, while trying to give the impression that none of it made any sense. When he hung up and turned to me his face was somewhat grim, his pale blue eyes filled with a rueful light.

'Well, that's it, I'm afraid,' he said. 'It's business for me today; our outing will have to be postponed.'

'Is it your office again?' I queried.

'Yes, and they're becoming a flaming nuisance. But I have to go along with them because I'm due for promotion, and if I refuse to do these extra little services then I might get passed over.'

'Of course you must do it. I'll think of something else to do today and we can make our trip tomorrow.'

'Tomorrow will be all right.' He nodded. 'I hate leaving you in the lurch like this, but business is business. What about your Italian friend, what's-his-name?'

'Donato. I'm afraid he'll be busy for a few days.' I forced a smile. 'But I don't need an escort. I have been known to go around on my own, and I have no doubt it would be all too easy to find a willing guide out there on the streets.'

'Like your stocky Italian?' he cut in sharply, and my face sobered instantly.

'I think I'll use the car,' I mused. 'Perhaps I'll leave Rome altogether today. A trip to the coast would be nice. I've heard about the Ostia Lido.'

'But you can always spend a day on the beach back in England,' he protested.

'Ostia Antica then,' I continued imperturbably. 'There are some marvellous ruins there, I believe.'

He nodded slowly, his face showing disappointment. 'I wish I could go with you,' he said. 'What a nuisance this business is! I'm supposed to be on holiday.'

'Never mind. Just think — if you get promoted, you'll be able to spend all your time in Rome.'

'That's a thought. But I'm sorry if I've disappointed you. I must leave now. I'll take a taxi to the office.'

'See you later, then!' I kept my tone casual, as if I felt sorry for him but would not let his absence spoil my enjoyment. I didn't for one moment think that he was going to work. He probably had to see his criminal associates to plan their next robbery!

I watched him depart. He certainly acted the part of a disappointed man. I felt the receptionist's dark, intense gaze on me and looked at her. She stirred — she had been watching Paul intently.

'He's such a nice man!' she said.

I nodded, wondering if I could follow him in the Fiat. He still had not told me the name of his insurance company. I knew I should make the effort to find out more about his activities, as Donato had suggested, but suddenly I felt diffident about it, where before I had been eager to get to the bottom of the mystery. Now all I wanted to do was enjoy a little bit of my holiday.

'We had a good outing planned for today,' I said.

'Business before pleasure,' she countered, and I turned away, not wanting anything more of her deceit.

By the time I had the Fiat nosing out

of the courtyard into the street, there was no sign of Paul, and I clenched my teeth in frustration. I could almost wish that I had never met Paul Russell. I drove on, making for no particular destination, wondering if I should drive out to Ostia as I had told Paul. It seemed like a good idea. The distance was about twenty-four miles, and I suddenly felt like getting away from it all. Perhaps a change of scenery would give me respite from the teeming worries threatening to overwhelm me.

The thought no sooner occurred than I was acting upon it. I stopped at the kerb and scanned my maps. Ostia Antica, where the ruins were, was easily found. I needed to take the Autostrada called the Via del Mare, and drove on, sighing with relief as I turned left at the Colosseum, passed the railway station, and eventually found the highway I wanted.

My cares seemed to fall away as I left Rome, travelling westward. Relief began to swell in my mind, and I realised that

I had been dreadfully tense and worried without really being aware of the fact. I could only hope that the tension hadn't shown in my face earlier. Paul hadn't seemed suspicious of my manner and had seemed really disappointed that we couldn't be together today. But I reminded myself that he was a criminal; that there was no insurance company demanding his assistance in some business matter. His business, whatever it was, was illegal, and he was pursuing it at this very moment. If I had not been such an idiot, I would have managed to follow him and put myself out of the torment that seemed to grip me.

The miles passed quickly, and soon the little town of Ostia Antica appeared. I parked in a convenient spot, took my shoulder bag and camera, and went to view the sights. The town was encircled by the ruins of a ninth-century rampart. I found the details in my guidebook and read them avidly. A fifteenth-century fortress was adjoining, which had been built by Pope Julius II. The book remarked that Roman Ostia was one of the best preserved cities of antiquity, and I meant to discover if that was true.

I was moved by the beauty of the ruins despite the fact that my senses had been inundated during the past two days by the marvellous sights of Rome. But there was no air of desolation around this site as is so frequent in such places, because aromatic bushes, cypresses, and umbrella pines were growing profusely to relieve the stark outlines. The entrance to the excavations was not far from the railway station, and I noted a restaurant nearby with tables set out in the garden.

The city was at least a mile long and half a mile wide, and my legs were aching before I had half covered the area. But I pressed on, looking at tombs that lined a street, trying to glean some information from the Latin inscriptions on them. Then I came across the best-preserved and most interesting remains of the city — small houses almost intact, having stood the test of time. I forgot my troubles by delving into the past, and was surprised, when finally glancing at my watch, to discover that the morning was well and truly past.

There were a lot of tourists looking around, and I had taken some camera shots of various points of interest. But lunchtime was drawing most people to the restaurant, and I began to feel hungry. I wanted to take the weight off my feet and looked for a convenient spot to rest. There was a stretch of grass beside a low wall, and I sat down thankfully and eased off my shoes. I spent far too much time sitting at a typewriter, I told myself, and would have to make an effort when I returned to England to take regular exercise.

The sun lulled my senses, and I leaned back against the wall, closed my eyes, and drifted into sleep. I could hear the birds singing, and the faint breeze was hot against my cheeks. A sharp crack suddenly disturbed the peacefulness, and there was terrific thud close to my head — a strange sound that I could not identify. I opened my eyes and glanced around to my left, peering at a spot on the wall about a foot from my head where a little cloud of dust was drifting away from a deep mark from which small splinters of stone were dropping to the grass.

I blinked, my mind filled with startled curiosity. Again there was that ominous cracking sound, very much like a whip being used close by, and I saw a small piece of stone jerk out of the wall within two feet of my head. Dust flew, and something stung my right cheek. I froze, staring in horror, filled with incredulity. I had never been shot at before.

I looked around. There were no tourists to be seen. Then I spotted a movement almost opposite, and gasped when a big man stepped fully into view from a corner. He was big and broad-shouldered, dressed like a tourist in a blue-and-white checked shirt with navy-blue trousers and a camera suspended from his neck by its strap. More ominously, he was holding a small automatic pistol in his right hand. He glanced around, saw that we were alone, and then came across the narrow street towards me. I gazed at him in disbelief, a sense of unreality holding me paralysed.

He halted before me, pointing the gun at my head. I stared into the deadly muzzle, my eyes bulging in fear.

'Just sit still and listen,' he snarled in good English in a voice that sounded like gravel. He was Italian. His gaze flickered to the wall where the shots had struck. 'I think I've made my point clear. You can be killed at any time, anywhere, if it is wished. But no harm will come to you if you return to Rome, get your own car, and leave Italy at once. Do I make myself clear?'

When he paused for my reply I discovered that my tongue was stuck to the roof of my mouth, and I could only nod mutely. The gun in his hand was black — an automatic of small calibre, though it looked as large as a cannon to my unblinking gaze. I also noticed that the top of his right index finger was missing. There was a bulbous pad of flesh at the joint where it ended, and his middle finger was on the trigger.

'Well?' he demanded hoarsely. 'Do you get the message?'

I gulped. There was a lump in my throat, and the mere sight of the gun held me speechless. He nodded, a sadistic smile coming to his face.

'You're scared, all right! So just heed my warning. Get out of Rome today. The next time there won't be any warning. You'll get a bullet through your head and your body will be found floating in the Tiber. I'll leave now. You sit here for ten minutes before moving. I shall be watching you from cover, and if you attempt to talk to anyone before you get back to Rome I will know, and I'll kill you before anyone can help you.'

He glanced left and right. I saw two middle-aged tourists in the distance, but they were not coming my way. He nodded and turned on his heel, departing around the corner from which he had appeared. I sat motionless in a tight cocoon of fear, unable to move a muscle. When he had gone I found it difficult to believe the incident had occurred. I came out of my shock slowly and began to tremble uncontrollably. My heart thudded and my pulse raced. I felt ill. Even sitting down, my knees trembled.

I had an incredible impulse to scream, but I forced it down. That man, whoever he was, might well be watching me from cover, and I had no intention of disobeying him. Tears flooded my eyes. My shoulders were twitching, and I couldn't have got to my feet if my life depended upon it. I thought remotely how fortunate it was that he had ordered me to remain seated for ten minutes after his departure.

The moments passed by, and I began to recover from my terrible fright. But I was badly scared, and that was putting it mildly. A sigh gusted from me. I looked down at my trembling hands. But questions were beginning to flood into my mind. What was this all about?

The details of the whole mystery flashed through my head in an unnerving stream, and I found this latest development even more puzzling than anything that had gone before. My presence in Rome was clearly undesirable to someone, and yet my arrival had evidently been awaited. Was it because these criminals, whoever they were, had discovered that I was trying to aid the police? That seemed to be the likely answer. Someone must have followed Donato after he left me, after our trip to the Villa Borghese. Perhaps I had been seen following Paul and Rinaldi to that place they broke into.

The more I considered, the more likely that explanation seemed. Whatever they had planned in the first place, my meeting with Donato and his connection with the police had disconcerted them. But I had no intention of disobeying the grim instructions that had been given me. I was going back to Rome, and even if my car had not been repaired, I was taking it and heading back to England as fast as speed limits would permit.

When I finally got to my feet I had to lean against the wall until I regained my equilibrium. At first my legs refused to take my weight. I fought for control, and by degrees the nightmarish atmosphere dissipated, and the chill sensation in my breast and stomach began to relax. I walked unsteadily along the street, looking neither left nor right, and departed from the ruins. As I neared the Fiat, I wanted to run but forced myself to remain outwardly calm. My hunger was gone now, and all my instincts were prickling. Survival! It was the only thought in my mind.

I dropped the car keys as I tried to unlock the door, and had to fight hard to maintain my faltering control. I was badly scared. When I was seated behind the wheel I felt more secure, and risked a quick glance around, wondering where the man with the gun had gone, for he might still be watching me. I flinched as I imagined a stream of bullets smashing through the windscreen. Then I turned on the ignition, started the engine, and pulled away jerkily, my trembling foot awkward on the clutch. But the car moved on, and I drove back to Rome as quickly as I could.

As the miles dropped behind me, my panic eased and more rational thoughts returned to my mind. But I was breathless and my temples were throbbing heavily. Now I really had a headache! But more than that, I was really frightened for the first time in my life.

A blue car passed me, heading for Rome at a terrific speed, and I peered after it, wondering if it contained my assailant. He had been a complete stranger to me, and I realised there might be others. I had no way of knowing who was against me; they held all the advantages. But now I didn't care about the mystery. All I wanted to do was get out of Rome, as I had been ordered.

I felt steadier by the time I reached Rome, my fears practically under control. But I kept hearing in my mind the terrible thudding sound of those bullets striking the wall close to my head. They had not been intended to kill me, but their impact made me realise what a mess they could have made of my mere flesh and bone.

It was still early in the afternoon when I pulled into the courtyard of the hotel, and I sat in the car for several minutes while regaining my composure, though my legs still trembled as I alighted and walked across to the hotel entrance. Now there was just one thought in my mind: I wanted to get my own car back and get out of Rome.

The receptionist was in the lobby; I would have been surprised had she not been. I crossed to the desk and leaned against it.

'Are you feeling unwell?' she enquired. 'You're looking very pale.'

I wondered how she would have felt if she had gone through what I had experienced that morning, but said nothing. Instead, I opened my bag and produced the scrap of paper on which Donato had written his telephone number. I sagged as I handed it to the receptionist, and she tentatively reached out a hand as if to steady me.

'Would you get that number for me?' I asked.

She took the paper, glanced at it, and gazed at me for a moment before reaching for the telephone. A moment later she handed the receiver to me and I heard a woman's voice speaking in Italian at the other end of the line. Mindful of the fact that I was not supposed to understand Italian, I moistened my dry lips.

'Do you speak English?' I asked.

'Yes,' the anonymous voice replied immediately.

'I would like to speak to Donato, please.'

'Are you Gail Bennett?'

'Yes. How did you know?'

'Donato has told me about you. There is only one Englishwoman in his life, so he tells me. I am his sister Gina.

I'm sorry, Donato is not here at the moment, but he asked me to take a message if you should call.'

'Thank you. Would you ask him to come to the hotel to see me as soon as he can?'

'Yes, I will. I'm expecting him home about four. He'll come and see you immediately.'

'Thank you.' I almost dropped the receiver as I returned it to the receptionist.

'There's something about Rome that doesn't suit you,' she remarked, peering into my face.

I mentally agreed, and wondered if she knew exactly what was bothering me. She had more knowledge of this situation than anyone. It was her telephone conversation with that unknown person that had started off the whole mystery. But I was in no condition to confront her, and all I wanted to do was talk to Donato about getting out of Rome. I was going to heed the frightening warning I had been given. The Italian police could handle their own business; they were more accustomed to it. I intended to cut my holiday short and go back to where I belonged.

9

In the sanctuary of my room, I took some aspirin and lay down on the bed. The fact that I had eaten no lunch made me feel faint, but the fright I had received in the ruins at Ostia had put all thoughts of sustenance out of my head. I kept reliving that grim episode, scarcely able to accept that it had occurred. This was a nightmare from which I could not awaken. I longed for Donato to arrive. Even if my car was not ready, I was going to take it and get out of Rome. I had to draw the line somewhere. I hadn't liked sneaking on Paul, but when it came to violence and the use of guns it was time to disappear.

I drowsed a little, but could not sleep; and when there was a knock at the door I started up in alarm, sprang off the bed and hurried to stand by the wall beside the door.

'Who's there?' I called cautiously.

'It's Paul.'

I gulped at the lump that rose in my throat. Paul! I pictured his face. He was a criminal, like the man who had confronted me earlier. I did not know what was going on, but Paul and the frightening stranger were somehow linked by crime.

'Are you all right, Gail?' he demanded, and I knew by the sound of his voice that he was standing close to the door. Perhaps he had come to see if I was already packing to leave.

'Yes, I'm fine,' I replied. 'It's only a headache. I was trying to sleep.'

'When I came in the receptionist mentioned you were feeling ill. I've been busy all day. I wouldn't have disturbed you, but I was afraid you were really unwell.'

I knew I would be if I didn't get out of Rome, but I sighed and unbolted the door, opening it slowly. Paul's alert gaze swept past me, no doubt looking for Donato. Then he bent his attention on me.

'You certainly look peaky,' he observed. 'Perhaps you should see a doctor.'

'No, I don't need a doctor.'

'Where did you go this morning?'

I looked into his eyes, and if he knew anything at all about what happened to me that morning then he was a marvellous actor, for there was nothing showing in his face or eyes. He seemed genuinely concerned. Then it struck me like a thunderbolt — I had told him before we parted earlier that I intended to go to Ostia. So that was how the man with the gun knew where to find me!

'What's wrong?' he asked, reaching out and grasping my elbow. 'Are you sure you're all right?'

'Yes. There's nothing wrong with me. I didn't have any lunch, and that's probably made me feel faint.'

'Why didn't you?' His tone was sharp, and I was sure he was aware of the latest development.

'I didn't feel like it.'

'Oh!' For a moment he seemed nonplussed because my attitude was neither one thing nor the other. 'Have you made any plans for this evening?'

'Donato is coming here for me. I don't know exactly when — late afternoon or early evening.'

'Ah!' He nodded. 'Then I won't hang around. Have a nice evening.'

He turned and walked to his room, and I peered around before closing my door. When I went back to my bed my brow was furrowed, but instead of lying down and resting I got out my cases and began to pack. I was leaving Rome. Only a fool would ignore the menace of a gun and a man who was fully prepared to use it.

An hour later there was another knock at the door while I was finishing my packing. Again I stood to one side before calling, half-afraid that a volley of shots would come splintering through the woodwork. I had read of stranger things happening, and this time, instead of it happening to someone else, I was involved.

'Who is it?' I demanded.

'Donato!'

I unbolted the door. My relief was immense. Donato frowned as he looked into my face, and then held out his hands towards me.

'What is wrong, Gail? My sister said you sounded upset when you called her.'

'Come in.' I stepped aside to let him enter, and then peered around the corridor before closing the door. Emotion began to boil up inside me as I faced him, and I knew reaction was about to hit me hard. I explained what had occurred at Ostia and saw disbelief dawn on his face. He swallowed quickly, then clenched his hands. When I lapsed into silence, his dark eyes were wide and filled with shock.

'Are you serious?' he demanded.

'Do you think I would make up such a tale just to shock you?' I countered, holding up my hands, which were trembling violently. 'Look at me! I'm practically a nervous wreck! I was never more frightened in my whole life! Two bullets hit the wall within two feet of my head, and when he told me to get out of Rome he really meant it. Now, I want my car, Donato.' I pointed to the bed, where my luggage was packed. 'What isn't done on it can be fixed when I get back home. Just make sure the wheels and the brakes are all right. I'm leaving as soon as possible.'

'But you can't do that!' he protested. 'I've been talking with my friends in the police. They are making a plan to trap the criminals.'

'Well, good luck to them, but you can count me out. I'm leaving.'

'I can understand your panic,' he soothed. 'I would have been frightened if it had happened to me. But I promise that no harm will come to you, Gail. The police will protect you.'

'That's what you've already told me, but where was my protection this morning, when I really needed it? I looked into the barrel of a gun and didn't like it. I've tried to help the police, but I have a limit, and I'll tell you here and now that I passed mine this morning.'

'The man who threatened you with a gun,' he cut in. 'Was he missing half the index finger on his right hand?'

I stared at him in disbelief. 'Yes, he had lost part of his finger. But how do you know that?'

Donato saw my expression and laughed. 'He's not a friend of mine, if that's what you're thinking, and you won't be worried by him again. He's under arrest.'

'Under arrest?'

'He was caught speeding on the outskirts of the city. He is known to the police, also the car he drives. They stopped him as a matter of routine and found a gun hidden in his car. I saw him being questioned at the police station and made a note of his appearance. Now you've described him, and that's all the police will need to put him away for a very long time. I'd better call my friend and report what you've told me. Then you won't have to leave. Better still, I'll take you to meet a police officer this evening. He will be able to reassure you. And your car will be ready in about two days.'

'If my car is roadworthy then I want it tonight, Donato,' I said firmly. 'I plan to leave Rome as soon as I can. There'll be other men in that gang who I can't identify, and I'm certain they'll come after me.'

'Where is Russell?' Donato asked.

'He's in the dining room. I've just left him. He didn't turn a hair, and if he is aware of what's going on then he's a very good actor indeed. He was chatting so casually over tea, and yet this morning one of his associates was threatening me with a gun.'

'The police are interrogating that man right now,' Donato asserted. 'His name, by the way, is Giuseppe Monati, and he is suspected of being a member of Rinaldi's gang. Your experience with him today confirms the suspicions of the police. If you are ready we'll go to my house now, without your luggage, and you can talk to a member of the local police.'

I nodded. 'Very well! I've been given until tonight to get out of Rome. But let's hurry. Time is getting away.'

'If you still want to leave after you've spoken to the police I will let you have the use of the Fiat. We have a company in England and I will arrange for the car to be picked up from there, and your car will be shipped to you.'

'Thank you.' I began to feel relieved. At last I seemed to be making some progress.

Donato drove out of the courtyard. I could not help gazing around as we travelled along the street, half-expecting bullets to come splintering into the vehicle. My nerves were still badly shaken, and I tried to take a firm grip on them. I sensed that I was going to have nightmares for a long time to come.

We drove across the city and eventually entered the driveway of a beautiful villa. Wrought-iron gates stood open, and the car swung between their stone pillars at what seemed breakneck speed, indicating that Donato was accustomed to entering and departing. The doorway to the villa was also pillared, and the entrance hall had a mosaic floor. I was engrossed by the sumptuous appearance of the place, but recalled that Donato had mentioned that his family was wealthy. He led me to double doors and flung them open with a flourish, revealing a long, cool room.

A handsome uniformed figure was standing at one side of the window overlooking a garden. Tall and immaculately dressed, he wore khaki-coloured trousers and jacket, with a dark brown leather belt around his waist that supported a pistol holster. He came instantly to the centre of the room as we entered and paused there, a smile coming to his fine features as he bowed slightly.

'Tenenti Niccolo Madante, at your service,' he greeted me formally.

'Lieutenant Madante is a member of the Carabinieri,' said Donato. 'He has been handling this particular case from its beginning. When he learned what happened to you today he insisted on coming to see you personally.'

'I cannot speak such good English as Donato,' Madante said. He was in his thirties; handsome in that Latin way which in some women brings out the urge to flirt. He had a thick accent and spoke slowly. 'I wish to thank you for what you are doing, and to reassure you that there is no danger to you.'

'That's kind of you,' I replied, 'but I have decided to leave Rome tonight, and nothing you say will make me change my mind.' I glanced at Donato, whose face was expressionless.

'The man who threatened you is under arrest,' Madante said.

'So Donato told me, but he's not the one I'm worried about. It's the possibility that there might be others in the gang that scares me. The police can't protect me all the time, and if those criminals are determined to get me then they'll pick their time and place, and that will be that as far as I am concerned. I'll be found floating in the Tiber, so the man said. No, Lieutenant Madante, I have done more now for the police than anyone has a right to expect from a member of the public, and you will have to complete this case with no further help from me.'

'There is nothing more for you to do,' Madante said with a smile, his dark eyes gleaming. 'The information we have gained from Monati will help us close the case. It is just a matter now of setting a trap when the gang strikes again so we can round them up. I merely want to reassure you that there is no further danger. My officers are out now, picking up suspects. I am certain we shall have all the members of the gang under arrest before the night is over. So you can go ahead and enjoy the rest of your holiday.'

'What about Rinaldi and Russell?' I demanded.

'They are the main ones in this, and we must leave them until we can discover where they have hidden the jewellery their gang has stolen. They will not harm you. They are too closely watched now. I will tell you that some members of their gang disagreed with the plan to involve you in transporting the stolen jewellery. That is why Monati set out to frighten you at Ostia. He wanted you to leave Rome because he was afraid that we were getting too close. Donato was followed from your hotel yesterday by one of the gang, and was seen to enter the police station where I have my office. We should have been more careful, but the gang are nervous, and sought to put us off by getting rid of you.'

'I see!' His words cleared up some of the mystery, but I was not satisfied. 'When you said they wanted to get rid of me, did you mean they wanted me to leave Rome, or were they planning to kill me? Monati actually said I would be floating in the Tiber.'

'He told me he was bluffing. All he wanted was for you to leave Rome and be of no further help to the police.'

I relived the moment when I had gazed into the steady muzzle of the gun, and didn't feel sure that Monati hadn't meant what he said.

'Your experience would have scared the most fearless of men,' Madante said. 'It was most unpleasant. But Monati is behind bars and will remain there for several years. I shall need a statement from you regarding the incident at Ostia, and then you can settle down to enjoying the rest of your holiday.'

Madante's words heartened me and I began to have second thoughts, but I had experienced a terrific shock and I was still fearful. I didn't think I could ever feel easy in Rome after what had happened. And Paul and Rinaldi were still at liberty! Obviously they were not on the side of the criminals who wanted the get rid of me, but there were still many details I did not know and a host of questions clamouring in my mind that needed answering. I looked from Donato to Madante, and saw that both were watching me intently, awaiting my reaction.

'Have you told me everything?' I asked. 'Or is there something else you want me to do?'

'You have done too much already, as you pointed out,' replied Madante. 'We do not have the right to expect more. It is our problem, not yours, and yet you could still be of great service to us. There is a link between Paul Russell, Rinaldi and another that is unknown to us. If you could spend more time with Russell perhaps he would unwittingly lead you to that anonymous man.'

'I don't really have the time to do what you ask,' I replied, shaking my head. 'I'm a working woman and I've wasted a lot of my time already. I couldn't possibly go through with what you have in mind. And it's too much of a strain trying to keep up appearances in Paul's company.' I glanced appealingly at Donato. 'Have a heart! I've done all I can.'

'It would be a pity if they escaped

with the jewellery,' Donato said, shaking his head. 'But I do agree with you. If you are not willing to help the police further then you should be permitted to do your own thing.'

'Very well.' Madante nodded. He held out his hand to me. 'I thank you sincerely for what you have done. You have been most public-spirited. Donato will see to it that you enjoy the rest of your holiday.'

'Thank you.' I shook hands with him.

Donato took my arm. 'We'll go now,' he said. 'Niccolo will leave shortly by the rear entrance. He does not want anyone to see him here. But now you can forget all about this business. I'm going to take you out to dinner at one of the finest night clubs in Rome. Does that appeal to you?'

'It sounds wonderful, but not this evening, Donato. I'm still badly shaken, and I don't think my nerves will settle until I've had a good night's sleep.'

'Very well! I'll drive you back to the hotel. You will still have the use of the

Fiat until your car is repaired.'

'Thanks, but I'll drive myself to save you the trouble of taking me all the way and then having to catch a taxi back here.'

'Who am I to argue with a beautiful woman?' Donato smiled. 'When shall I see you again? Perhaps I may call for you first thing in the morning? I shall have to go to Florence soon for a few days.'

I smiled at the lieutenant, who bowed, and Donato escorted me out to the car. He took hold of my hands and squeezed them gently.

'You have been a very brave woman, Gail. You will never know just how much you have helped, and I am so sorry you had to experience that frightening situation at Ostia. It was quite unexpected.'

'All's well that ends well,' I said, smiling despite the shock that still gripped me. I sighed and opened the car door. 'I'd better get back to the hotel now. I think I need to do some writing. That usually has a calming effect on my nerves. Call me in the morning, Donato, and we'll talk about sight-seeing.'

He kissed me, a brotherly kiss, and I smiled and got into the car. I appreciated his sensitivity, for most men would not have realised that at the moment the last thing I wanted right now was love and tenderness. I was too wound up to have room for anything but fear in my mind.

I drove back to the road and paused to look around before continuing. There was hardly any traffic at that moment, but there was a parked car some twenty yards to the right of the gateway; and as I passed it, I recognised it. Rinaldi's car! I gazed at it worriedly as I drove on, and when I looked in the rear-view mirror I saw it pull away from the kerb and begin to follow me.

Two figures were in the car. Rinaldi was driving, and I recognised Paul beside him in the front passenger seat. Panic flooded me and for a few minutes

I hardly knew what I was doing. I fought down the immediate impulse to turn the car and rush back to Donato. That was not the answer to the situation. I kept driving, fighting for composure, and continued to the hotel, craving the sanctuary of my room.

But it seemed that I was worrying in vain, for Rinaldi suddenly accelerated, passed me and sped away into the distance, and when I glanced at the car as it went by I was surprised to see only Rinaldi inside. Then it dawned on me — Paul must have ducked down in his seat to avoid being seen by me. Despite my fears I smiled, because they were not aware that I could recognise Rinaldi's car.

Yet it was a frightening situation, with strange undercurrents tugging at my subconscious mind. I could not even guess how it would end, but Paul was obviously doomed to a long term of imprisonment, which saddened me; for despite what had happened, I still had feelings for him.

When I pulled into the courtyard of the hotel and parked the Fiat I was limp with relief, but as I alighted from the car I received yet another shock. Paul was sitting at the table on the little terrace, and he arose with a friendly smile as I approached the steps. I drew a deep breath and steeled myself for the encounter. His deceit was nothing less than audacious, and I had to fight sudden anger, for my natural reaction was to confront him with what I knew and put him firmly in his place.

But I could not reveal anything, because the police wanted to trap him, and the less he knew the easier would be their task. Contenting myself with the knowledge that he would be caught in the end, I smiled as I faced up to him. I had to play a role just as he was doing, and I had to be as good as he appeared to be.

10

'Has Donato stood you up?' asked Paul in a friendly manner, and his deceitfulness grated against my nerves. He was spoiling my entire holiday, trying to involve me in his crookedness, although I could not for the life of me see how he meant to do it. There was no way he could persuade me to help him in his criminal activities, and if he was thinking that he could, he had badly underestimated me.

'No, he has to go to Florence for a few days. It's important business that won't wait, so he said.'

For the first time since I had known him, I saw Paul lose his composure. His expression changed abruptly and pure shock gleamed in his eyes, but he recovered his poise instantly and I heard him sigh heavily. He smiled, but he looked like a man about to be hanged.

'His loss should be my gain.' He spoke lightly, smiling, but I could see that his manner was forced. 'May I have the pleasure of your company this evening?'

'It's kind of you to offer, but I've had a most trying day. I need to sit down in my room and bring my notes up to date and do some writing, which always settles my nerves. I'm rather relieved that Donato is going away, because I don't feel like going out this evening.'

'Donato must have something I haven't got,' he said ruefully. 'You went out with him even though you didn't feel like it, but I'm not such a powerful draw as him, is that it?'

'You sound just a little bit jealous.' I gave a tinkly laugh, fighting down my irritation. Why was he trying to involve me in his schemes?

'Jealous?' he repeated, smiling slowly. 'I'm just a lonely man, and we seemed to get along so well.'

'It isn't a good holiday as far as I'm concerned,' I retorted, wanting to put him in his place. 'I'm not anti-social, but I did tell you at the outset that I had to work and needed to be alone to do just that.'

'So you did, but Donato crashed into your life and you didn't seem to mind his company.'

I sighed and turned away, pretending weariness, and entered the hotel, leaving him standing on the terrace. There was a mixture of conflicting emotions in my mind. A part of me wanted to see Paul and was trying to blot out the ugly truth of the situation, and another part was forcing me to stay angry about the way he had been planning to use me. But the real pain came for being aware that he had affected me deeply in our short acquaintance, and I really wanted to see more of him.

The receptionist was at her desk. I swept by her and was almost at the foot of the stairs before she could look up and note my passing. But I was in no mood to exchange pleasantries with her, for she had duped me as well, pretending friendship after passing on information about me. And even Donato had used his meeting with me to get me working for the police.

Frustration boiled inside me, and my fear diminished in the face of my anger. But I locked myself in my room and settled down with my notebooks. I didn't feel the slightest inclination to work, but forced myself into the right frame of mind for it. I even told myself that I would profit from all of this. I could begin to write that novel I had always promised to tackle, using the characters I had met here in Rome. There was scope for a good story, but I needed to know more about Paul and his schemes before attempting a detailed plot.

I made copious notes for almost two hours before putting down my pen and flexing my fingers. But a sense of satisfaction gripped me. I had made a start; and having broken the ice, so to speak, the work had become easier. I arose from my bed, carefully put away my notebooks, and then crossed to the window and looked out at the beautiful Roman evening. In place of my previous anger, a sense of wistfulness now suffused me. I was on holiday but I was not happy. When I returned to England there would be a whole year of hard work awaiting me — endless assignments that were already planned, interviews, short stories to write, and new assignments to work up. If I couldn't find any pleasure in the next week or so, then I would miss out altogether this year.

Dissatisfaction gnawed at my mind. The room was hot and airless, and I felt the impulse to go for a drive before darkness settled in. But I remained at the window, for Rinaldi had suddenly appeared on the street below. I eased back to avoid being seen, wondering if he was waiting to see Paul or merely wanted to keep an eye on me. The answer to that unuttered question soon became apparent, for a few moments later Paul appeared in the courtyard and walked casually towards the exit.

I grabbed my shoulder bag and the car keys and was halfway down the stairs before I realised that I was no longer interested in what Paul Russell was doing in Rome. But if that was so, then why was I in such a hurry to follow him? I compressed my lips and continued, slowing my progress when I reached the lobby so as not to arouse the receptionist's interest. She was reading a magazine, but I saw her gaze flicker up and take me in. I knew she missed nothing that went on in the hotel; perhaps that was why she spent so long at that desk of hers.

The street outside the hotel was almost deserted, and I kept an eye on the part of it I could see as I went to the Fiat. It was as well that I did, for Rinaldi's car went by, and I slid hurriedly behind the wheel of the Fiat and switched on the ignition. In a matter of seconds I had backed out, turned the car, and was nosing into the street. Perhaps Paul and Rinaldi were going to collect their cache of stolen jewellery, or move it to a safer place. My pulse raced at the thought of being able to tell Donato that I knew where their loot was hidden.

Rinaldi's car was up ahead of me, and a black-and-green taxi pulled in between us. I followed easily, finding that I was becoming adept at shadowing another car. I had to stay well behind for fear of discovery, aware that men like Paul and Rinaldi would instinctively remain alert, like wild animals. The evening was well advanced, and soon darkness would begin to creep into the streets. It would cover my presence but make my self-imposed task that much more difficult.

Again they made for the outskirts of Rome, but seemed to have no particular destination. Once I feared that they had spotted the Fiat and Paul had recognised it, and that they were just leading me around on a wild-goose chase. But I came to the conclusion that they were waiting for darkness to fall, and despite my earlier denials to Donato and Lieutenant Madante, I could feel excitement crawling through my veins. Perhaps I ought to have joined the police back home instead of settling for the life of a writer.

Eventually Rinaldi's car entered a wide avenue and stopped at the kerb. I almost turned in behind them but saw they were stopping in time to keep moving along the street that intersected the avenue. I parked around the corner from them and quickly alighted, moving back to where I could see them and observe their movements. Rinaldi's car was motionless at the kerb, about fifty yards from me, and it was parked opposite an imposing villa. The lights of the car had been switched off, and I frowned as I wondered what to do next.

The shadows of night were deepening as I sneaked forward through the gloom, keeping to the shrubbery that lined the inside edge of the pavement. Paul was seated nearest the kerb, his window half-open, but the sound of the car radio came floating on the night air and I could hear their voices only as a low muttering in the background. I realised that they had probably switched on the radio in order to confuse eavesdroppers. Apparently there were no lengths to which these men were not prepared to go in order to further and protect their illegal business. But some scraps of their conversation reached my ears, particularly between the pauses in the music.

I sighed when I heard Paul's voice, but could not understand what he said. Rinaldi made some reply. They were speaking Italian. Then I heard Rinaldi's voice as the music cut out, and strained to pick up his words.

'If we're not careful the whole plan will fall through,' said Rinaldi. 'I don't like using Gail Bennett; your association with her is dangerous, Paul.'

'Everything is developing as we hoped,' Paul replied, and I craned closer, eager to learn all I could. 'The other side are using her, so why shouldn't we? But her manner toward me has changed over the past day or so.'

'Perhaps it is the charm of di Barocci!' Rinaldi chuckled.

Their voices faded again as Rinaldi, fiddling with tuning the radio, changed stations and louder music blotted out all other sounds. I felt numb as I sneaked back the way I had come. If I needed proof that I was being used, or at least figured in their schemes as an unwitting assistant, then that was it. I fought against the anger that threatened to explode inside me, for if I lost control then very likely I would go back to Rinaldi's car and confront the crooked pair. But the incident at Ostia was still vibrant in the background of my mind; I knew they were ruthless men and that I had to be very careful.

Night was closing in quickly now, and I was able to get back to the Fiat without much danger of being seen by Paul or Rinaldi, even if they were keeping a keen eye on their surroundings. I wondered about the villa they were so obviously watching. Were they planning another robbery?

I turned the corner and walked faster to the Fiat. There was another car now parked behind it, and I barely gave it a glance as I stopped at the car and fumbled with the key. I heard a sharp sound as of a car door being thrust open, and looked round quickly. A man, shapeless in the gloom, was getting out of the other car, and I felt an intuitive pang. For some unaccountable reason I hurriedly opened the car door, but a strong hand grasped my shoulder; and as I was spun around, another hand clamped across my mouth. I tried to scream, but the cruel fingers were cutting off my air, and for a frightening moment I feared that I would be suffocated on the street.

There was no talking. Everything happened quickly and silently, as if it had been rehearsed. I was bundled into the back of the Fiat and someone started the engine. The car lurched away from the kerb as I struggled against the powerful hands holding me. They tightened their merciless grip and I was forced down on the seat. A coat was flung over my head and shoulders, and then I felt the hard ring of a gun muzzle pressing against my back. A harsh voice spoke in poor English: 'Do not make a sound. Stay still and be quiet.'

The hands released me then, but the muzzle of the gun remained pressed against my spine, and I lay motionless, filled with anguish at my foolhardiness. I ought to have got out of Rome when I had the opportunity earlier. But that is the cry of the heroine in almost any murder or crime story — 'if only'! However, in my case it was real, and the renewed shock and fear I now felt were ten times worse than that which I'd experienced at Ostia when confronted by Monati. I had thought that was bad enough, but now I knew better, and it was too late.

The most frightening thing of all was the silence. All I could hear of my captors was heavy breathing coming from the man who had grabbed me, and the size of his hands warned that he was powerful. There were several men — at least two in the Fiat with me, and one in the car they had used to get close to me. I was in a real spot, and I dared not contemplate my immediate future. I was in the clutches of the gang while Paul and Rinaldi were sitting calmly in their car. Perhaps they were not even watching the villa! It was possible they knew I would follow them — maybe they had seen me on the previous occasion — and planned the whole thing. I was the fly in the spider's web, and yet it all seemed so unreal. But what were they going to do with me?

I thought of Donato's assurances, and Lieutenant Madante telling me there was no danger, but here I was up to my sweet neck in trouble. The coat over my head was suffocating, and I fought down my panic, knowing that I had to retain my control. I lifted my left hand and tried to move the heavy cloth, and the strong hands tightened their grip yet again. The thick voice spoke quickly, warning me to remain still.

'I can't breathe!' I gasped angrily.

'Let her up but keep her covered,' another voice snapped.

The coat was removed, and I drew a deep breath into my palpitating lungs. The interior of the Fiat was oppressively hot. Shadows filled the back of the car, but when I tried to turn my head to look at my captors, strong fingers closed around my neck and kept my face averted.

'Stay still and perhaps you will live a little longer,' the harsh voice said, and again the gun muzzle was jabbed against my spine.

'What is the meaning of this?' I snapped. 'Am I being kidnapped? If you hope to hold me for ransom then you've made a big mistake. I have no money. I am a British subject. You had better let me go.'

Both men in the car laughed harshly,

and my blood seemed to freeze in my veins as I listened.

'You were told to leave Rome but you have ignored the warning. So what did you expect to happen?'

'You're making a mistake,' I said.

'We never make mistakes,' came the grim reply. 'Now be quiet.'

There was such raw menace in the tone that I forgot my anger. What were they going to do with me? That was the question I felt I did not want to be answered at that moment. I was terribly afraid but tried not to show it, and lay on the back seat trying to keep my panic under control and my mind working normally. I could not see out of the windows and had no idea where we were going, but when the trip ended I would probably learn the answers to some of the questions that had been bothering me ever since I booked in at the hotel. It was also likely that those answers would not be to my liking.

After some minutes of complete silence, my fear subsided a little. Just how many men were there in this gang? Lieutenant Madante had said suspects were being arrested, but there were several men involved in my kidnapping. Had the police been fooled into believing that some other gang was responsible? It was possible, and if that were so then I was in rather a bad situation. I fought against rising hysteria. Surely these men would not kill me in cold blood! Madante had said there was no danger of that happening; it wasn't the way thieves operated. Now, lying in the back of the car with a gun stuck against my spine, I was not so sure I could accept the lieutenant's theory.

My only hope was Donato, but I did not see how he could help. He had no knowledge of my whereabouts or predicament, and probably imagined that I was back at the hotel. He wouldn't be calling for me there until tomorrow morning, and by then I might be dead.

The car suddenly braked; I was almost flung off the seat. There were epithets in Italian. The man in the front passenger seat cursed at the driver, who replied in similar manner. I eased up slightly, peered through a window, and was unable to recognise my surroundings. It was clear, at least, that we were still in Rome, and not on the outskirts. A traffic policeman was holding up the vehicles at a crossroads. His back was to us, and he had halted the Fiat to beckon an ambulance on from the right. The gun muzzle prodding my back bored even harder, making me squirm, and I glanced at the pale blur of the face beside me.

'You stay quiet,' he rasped, and I gulped at the lump in my throat. The engine of the car was running sweetly, and the surrounding silence seemed to pile up. The men were growing more nervous by the minute. Finally, the cop turned and beckoned us on.

The gun muzzle dug at my back as the car went forward. But the driver stalled the car and the man at his side cursed ferociously. Behind us a car hooted impatiently, and suddenly it felt to me that the whole grim situation was falling to pieces.

The cop was looking at us, motioning impatiently for the driver to get moving. The car was restarted and moved forward jerkily. I thought the policeman was going to stop us. He did not move out of the path of the car until the very last moment, and then peered intently into the shadowed interior.

'You fool!' snapped the man beside me in Italian. 'What are you trying to do, get yourself arrested? A child could handle the car better than you.'

'You can talk,' the driver replied. 'I think we are in a lot of trouble now and I don't like any of it. We are making mistake after mistake. It's about time we got down to business and finished things off.'

'Shut up!' cut in the man in the front passenger seat. 'The woman is listening, remember.'

'Our information is that she does not speak or understand Italian,' snapped the driver.

I could guess where he had got that

information from, and if I ever got the opportunity to confront the hotel receptionist again I'd know what to say and do. I realised now that I had been a fool not to tell Donato everything from the very beginning. If he had had any idea at all that the receptionist was also involved, then the police could have questioned her. But it was too late now. My immediate fate was uncertain, and I was scared to death. Hope was all I had left. There was no chance of escaping from these men, and they seemed to know what they were doing. They were professional criminals, and obviously very successful, I imagined, judging by the way they ignored the police. I sat motionless, stiff with dread, as the car went on to some unknown destination. When the trip ended it was possible that my life would end with it.

11

When the car stopped again, we were under trees that grew beside the wall of a large villa. A driveway wound from the building to the road. I could not even see the gateway as I was hustled out of the car and in through a side door. Three men surrounded me, and they were ominously silent as I was ushered up a flight of stairs. It suddenly came to me through a cloud of fear that the house was bare of furniture, and there was an air of desolation inside. My footsteps echoed. There were no lights on. One of the men was carrying a torch, but its dancing beam failed to penetrate the black shadows that swirled menacingly about us.

'What are you going to do with me?' I demanded, trying to muster up some nerve.

'Perhaps you would not be happy

with an answer to that question,' was the frightening reply. 'This villa is isolated, and you could scream to your heart's content, but no one could possibly hear you. However, one of us will always be around, and if you cause any disturbance you will be dealt with.'

I didn't like the sound of that and maintained my silence. We went along a wide corridor to the rear of the building, and one of them opened a door, then pushed me unceremoniously into a small room. The door was slammed and I stood alone in the darkness, peering around, trying to make out details of my surroundings. Starlight filtered in through a tall window. I moved forward cautiously until I could reach out and touch the glass. There were thick bars on the outside. When I tried to open the window it would not budge; and I could see nothing of the garden, for trees obstructed my view.

Turning slowly, I looked around the room, my eyes now accustomed to the shadows. I saw a single bed and some furniture. Crossing to the bed, I sat down gingerly and sighed heavily, feeling sorry for myself. I was also angry at the way I was being treated, which bolstered me against the full horror of this nightmare. But the uncertainty of my future was overwhelming. I was alone, in the clutches of desperate criminals. But I could not sit and wait patiently for whatever fate was being planned for me — I had to at least make an effort to escape.

Arising, I went to the door and tried the handle. It turned under pressure, but the door was obviously locked, bolted, or fastened on the outside. I had heard no sounds in the building after I had been locked in, but one of the men had said that at least one of them would be within earshot. That meant they were going to hold me prisoner for a period, either short or long, and whatever I was going to do to help myself would have to be done quickly. I arose from the bed, determined to try anything.

But it was soon clear that there was nothing I could do. I was locked in the room. The door was solid and the window was barred. Shouting for help would only bring one of my captors, and might precipitate my end.

I sat down again. Time was immeasurable. The very silence that surrounded me was heavy and ominous. I could hear the sound of blood throbbing in my temples. My nerves were stretched to breaking point. Only the knowledge that I would attract the wrong kind of attention prevented me from panicking.

Getting to my feet, I looked again for anything that might help me escape. If there was only one man in the house, then I should be a fool to resign myself to whatever my captors had in mind. If I could do something unexpected, then I might succeed in escaping.

There was a straight-backed wooden chair standing beside the door. I picked it up. It was heavy and solid. If there was just one man left guarding me, and I could entice him into the room . . . It would take courage, and the fear of attempting it outweighed my worry that it might fail. But I told myself that I had nothing to lose, except my life, and that was forfeit now. There was no one else who could help me.

I knocked on the door until my knuckles hurt without evoking any kind of response. I listened intently for seemingly endless minutes, and heard nothing. The continuing silence gave me heart, and I kicked the door determinedly, increasing the force when there was still no reply. I was keyed up to use violence; but no one appeared, and I eventually fell back in exhaustion. I went back to the bed and dropped heavily upon it, filled with growing despair.

Suddenly I heard a grating sound, saw the door swinging open, and froze, fearing the worst. I couldn't even reach the chair I had decided to use as a weapon. A figure appeared, cloaked in shadow. I shrank down on the bed.

'Gail?' Donato spoke huskily. 'Are you in here? Was it you knocking?'

'Donato?' The sound of his voice only added to my shock. The last person I expected to see was Donato. I sprang up from the bed and flung myself into his arms as I burst into tears, overcome by relief.

'Don't cry,' he consoled me. 'We told you no harm would come to you. The police have been watching your movements closely. They saw you being abducted, followed the gang here, and you were making so much noise you held the attention of the criminals until the police could get into the house.'

I dropped my head to his broad shoulder, gasping in relief. 'Oh, Donato, you'll never know how frightened I was!'

'Never mind. It is almost finished now. I'll take you back to the hotel. You'll be quite safe; it will be under police surveillance. I have to go to Florence tonight for at least two days, but you can be certain that nothing will happen to you while I'm away.'

As he spoke he led me from the room, and we descended the stairs.

There were still no lights anywhere, and as I tried to pierce the shadows I was still afraid that some unknown gang member would leap out at me. When we reached the entrance hall I saw a dim light showing through a half-open doorway. Donato led me into the room, and I saw Lieutenant Madante and two uniformed policemen guarding the three sullen-faced men who had abducted me. The trio had their hands raised and the policemen were menacing them with drawn guns.

'I will take Gail back to the hotel now, Lieutenant,' said Donato in English.

'I apologise for tricking you yet again into being of more help to me,' Madante said, coming toward the door. 'But as you see, we now have the rest of the gang, with the exception of the two leaders, who have knowledge of the whereabouts of a great deal of jewellery and cannot be arrested until after they have led us to their booty. Go now and put all of this out of your mind.'

'I don't think I shall recover from this

experience,' I said quickly, feeling angry at having been used yet again. But it was over now and there seemed no point in making a fuss. I looked into Donato's shadowed face. 'Please take me back to the hotel. I want to lock myself in my room and try to sleep. I'm exhausted.'

We left the villa. The Fiat was standing in the driveway. Donato ushered me in, then slid behind the wheel. I suppressed a shudder as he drove away from the grim, bleak building.

'That place,' I remarked, 'is it abandoned? There was no furniture except in the room where I was held prisoner.'

'It was being used by the gang, but the police were aware and were watching it. Lieutenant Madante did not want to move in too soon, but when it was discovered that you had been taken he could not hold back any longer.'

'Just in case they turned violent,' I added with a shiver.

'Exactly, but you're in no danger now. Russell and Rinaldi are under observation, and they cannot make a move without the police knowing about it. As soon as they collect the stolen jewellery they will be arrested. You see the problem facing the police?'

'Yes, and they have my sympathy, but I have no wish to be further involved in the business.'

'I agree. Unfortunately I must go to Florence as soon as I've dropped you at the hotel. I should have left earlier, but I stayed when I heard that the gang had abducted you. I will take the Fiat with me, and tomorrow morning your car will be delivered to you at the hotel. If you are out when it arrives, the keys will be left with the receptionist.'

'Will I see you again?' I looked at his face, noting his strong features in the dim light coming from the instrument panel. He glanced at me, and his teeth glinted when he smiled.

'Most certainly. I shall get my business over with as quickly as possible and return to Rome to ensure that you have the most wonderful holiday.'

'I won't feel easy until Paul Russell and Rinaldi have been arrested,' I said. 'And how can I face Paul and pretend nothing has happened? He'll know his men kidnapped me tonight.' I explained how I had followed them from the hotel earlier.

Donato nodded. 'I was told about that, and a police car picked me up. Other cars were following you at a distance. You were not in any real danger at all, but you didn't know that, and it must have been quite an ordeal for you.'

A chill gripped me when I recalled how I had been prepared to use violence to escape earlier. We lapsed into silence, but my thoughts seemed to run in circles. When we reached the hotel I began to think of how to steel myself for my next meeting with Paul. He knew what was going on, and yet acted as if nothing was wrong. Did he think I was too naïve to put two and two together?

We alighted from the car and I

looked quickly around the courtyard, searching for Paul, but he was not around. Donato clasped my hand, leaned sideways and kissed my cheek. Then he got back into the Fiat and drove off. I watched him until his tail-lights disappeared, then sighed heavily. I needed a shower and then my bed, too exhausted to consider any other course of action.

The shadows of the courtyard scared me; I was half-expecting someone to spring out at me. Shivers were running up and down my spine as I hurried to the terrace, still glancing around for Paul, for he had a habit of waylaying me. I didn't really want to see him again. But perhaps he expected that I was still being held prisoner by the rest of his gang. I wondered what his reaction would be when he returned to the hotel and learned that I was here.

When I entered the lobby, there was a surprise waiting for me: the receptionist was not at her desk. While I had been locked in that empty villa I had vowed to do something about her, but now I realised that I could not jeopardise the work of the police; and that fact would prevent me from facing down Paul as well. I shrugged my shoulders and went up to my room. It was no longer any of my business, and I wanted nothing more to do with the case. All I craved was to be left alone.

My relief was enormous when I finally entered the room and bolted the door. A nervous reaction set in and my legs seemed to turn to water and I staggered to the bed and sank down on it. I lay on my back, shivering. But I was made of sterner stuff, and after a few minutes I pushed myself erect and prepared to take a shower.

The hot jets of water refreshed my mind as well as my body, and afterwards I towelled myself off briskly; then I tumbled into bed. The bliss of losing consciousness, and with it all my fears and shock, filled me with the greatest sense of relief that I had ever experienced. I slept dreamlessly.

* * *

The next morning I awakened with the sunshine peeping in through the window. For some moments I drowsed luxuriously, thinking about the incidents that had overtaken me the previous day. There were so many facts of which I was unaware, and these missing pieces prevented me from seeing a true picture of what was happening. But then I cleared my mind — I was finished with all that. All I needed to do was keep out of Paul's way. If I never saw him again it would be too soon. But the thought brought pain, for I was involved with him whether I liked it or not. He had somehow crept into my heart and installed himself in an unassailable niche.

I put on a bold front and went down to breakfast, and now I experienced a sense of security. The gang was under arrest, and I did not think Paul would try to harm me.

The receptionist was at her desk, and as I approached her she held out my own car keys. I took them in surprise.

'A man delivered the Corsa about ten minutes ago,' she reported. 'I have looked it over, and they've done a very good job on it. There's no sign of any damage.'

'Thank you.' I went to the door and peered out across the courtyard, and there was the Corsa, parked near the entrance. It looked immaculate. I went out to it, filled with childish pleasure. But as I walked around the car to check the rear, where all the damage had occurred, I got a shock — for I discovered Paul squatting beside a rear wheel, examining it intently. He looked up at my approach and straightened, smiling pleasantly.

'Good morning,' he greeted me. 'I was just checking the work that has been done. It's first-rate. There's not a scratch anywhere, and you've got four new tyres, and two new wheels on the back.'

'Donato said he would make it like new,' I said. 'I can't believe it was ever in an accident.'

Paul ran a hand over the lid of the boot. 'They've done a beautiful job. Do you know that you have to report any repairs that have been done while the car is out of Britain?'

'Donato said something about giving me a certificate to that effect,' I said in a neutral tone. Paul turned his penetrating gaze on me. I compressed my lips and tried to look casual, but my heart was thudding as if I had just run up a flight of stairs. I hoped he was not aware of how he affected me. I turned and went back into the hotel, and was surprised to see when I paused at the door and looked back that Paul had not followed me. Then I forced my thoughts away from him, aware that it was in my mind to tell him that he was close to being arrested and should make a run for it. I did not want to help a criminal escape from the law, but I could not look on Paul as a crook.

After breakfast I went up to my room, checked my street guide, made plans for the day, and took my shoulder bag and camera. I was half afraid on my way down to the car that Paul might waylay me, but there was no sign of him. It was a pleasure to drive the Corsa again, and I could not fault its performance. Donato had certainly been as good as his word. A lot of work had been put into it during the short time it had been in his father's garage. I drove out of the courtyard and felt anxious for the first few minutes, looking out for Rinaldi's car, but it was not around; as I drew away from the area, I began to relax. Now, perhaps, I could get down to some serious work.

It was a pleasant, relaxing day. I looked over St Peter's, and soon lost myself in the crowd sight-seeing around the magnificent church. My first impression of the interior was unforgettable, and when I took the lift up to the base of the dome the view of Rome stole my breath away.

By lunch-time I was hungry, and found a small café that served wonderful food. This was more like the holiday

I had envisaged, and I was so engrossed in my surroundings that I completely forgot about Paul and Rinaldi. I made lots of notes, and my fingers were cramped by the time I called it a day — almost half a notebook was filled with shorthand.

Returning to the car, I felt a sense of deep satisfaction. At last I had managed to get some work done, and I was filled with the desire to expand the notes I had taken. But I planned to mix business with pleasure, and with no one around to distract me I could get up to date with what I had to do.

A man was sitting on a bench close to where the Corsa was parked, and as I unlocked the car door he got up and came to my side, his action rekindling my old fears. I stepped back from him as she spoke.

'Hello. I have been watching you. You're English, aren't you?'

'I'm in a hurry,' I replied, trying to move around him to open the door of the car. When he stepped sideways to block my movement I looked up quickly, wondering if he was one of Paul's gang.

'Are you staying long in Rome?' he continued.

I shook my head and put a hand on his arm to push him away from the car door. His response was to grasp my elbow, and I twisted away sharply, breaking his grip. He inadvertently moved away from the door and I pulled it open. At that moment I became aware of another man looming up, and stifled a gasp as I anticipated more trouble. I looked at the newcomer and was surprised to see it was Paul. He stepped forward and confronted the stranger, warning him in Italian to leave; and the man, after a regretful glance at me, went off reluctantly.

'It looked as if you were having some trouble, Gail,' said Paul, his eyes glinting like sapphires. A faint smile showed, but his jaw was set.

'Thank you,' I said awkwardly. 'He was becoming a nuisance. How did you happen to be here at such an opportune moment?'

'I had nothing to do today, so I've been following you around, keeping an eye on you.

'You've what?' My surprise was absolute.

'I told you that Rome isn't safe for an unaccompanied woman. I knew you wouldn't want me around, so I stayed in the background, and it looks as if my hunch has paid off. Anyway, you've been working really hard. That pen of yours has hardly stopped since you left the hotel. Are you satisfied with what you've got done?'

'Very!' I could feel a tingling sensation inside, and mentally struggled against my attraction to him. I thought of all that had occurred since I met him. He had deceived me and tried to involve me in his crooked plans, and he was still talking to me as if nothing had happened.

'Are you going back to the hotel now?' he asked.

'I am.'

'Would you give me a lift?'

'Certainly!' I could not believe that, whatever his business was, he would harm me; my intuitive belief was that I could not be safer with anyone else.

'What's it like, driving your own car again?'

'I'm feeling much happier now. It's surprising how one gets attached to a car.'

We got into the Corsa and I drove steadily back to the hotel, keeping my mind on the road and holding back innumerable questions that clamoured for answers.

'What are your plans for this evening?' he asked me.

'I don't have any, but I shan't be going out. I have some work to attend to. I have to develop some ideas and make some rough drafts.'

He nodded, his face expressionless; and when I turned into the courtyard of the hotel I could not help looking around for signs of Rinaldi. The small

Italian was nowhere to be seen. Paul got out of the car, and while I locked the vehicle he lightly ran his fingers over the new paintwork, nodding slowly as he examined it.

We entered the hotel and the receptionist called me over. Paul went on up to his room.

'There was a telephone call for you from Florence,' said the receptionist.

'Donato?'

'Yes. He said he will call again at seven.'

'I'll be here,' I told her.

I had already taken too many chances in the shadows of Rome's nights. Now nothing would induce me to leave the sanctuary of the hotel. I was restricted in my movements until Paul and the gang were under arrest, and the sooner Lieutenant Madante arranged that the better.

As I went up to my room to take a shower and change for the evening, I wondered about Paul. I could not get him out of my mind. He had followed me all afternoon, but I had not caught a glimpse of him, and Rinaldi had not shown himself either. Was that ominous? I had no way of telling, and waited impatiently for Donato to call. Perhaps he would have some good news for me.

12

At seven I was standing at the receptionist's desk. The telephone rang, and after answering, the receptionist held out the receiver to me. I smiled as I took it, but there was sudden tension inside me and I drew a sharp breath. Donato's voice sounded at the other end of the line.

'Hello, Gail.' His voice was strained, filled with concern. 'I'm on the point of leaving now. I've finished my business here and should be back in Rome by about eleven. How has your day been?'

'Fine.' I heard footsteps on the stairs and glanced over my shoulder to see Paul descending. He looked at me and, as our eyes met, his expression seemed to tighten. He came slowly towards the desk. I gulped, aware that although the receptionist had moved away, she was not quite out of earshot.

'Well, listen to me,' continued Donato. 'Whatever you do, stay away from Paul Russell. He could be dangerous. I left an address with Lieutenant Madante and he was in touch with me a short time ago. The police are almost ready to close in on Russell and Rinaldi, and will probably arrest them this evening. I think the best thing you can do is leave the hotel and drive around Rome until I get back, and then meet me at my home. Do you know the way there?'

'Yes, of course!' I frowned as I glanced at Paul. He had halted out of earshot and was obviously waiting for me to finish my call. 'I'll do what you say.'

'Now heed my warning,' repeated Donato. 'Don't go near Paul Russell. If he gets any idea that the net is closing in around him, he might grab you as a hostage. Please leave the hotel and stay away from all contacts until you come to meet me. As soon as Lieutenant Madante has made his arrests he will inform me, and then it will be safe for you again.'

'I'm ready to leave now,' I retorted heavily.

'What's wrong?' Donato asked. 'Are you not alone, Gail?'

'Not quite. But it's all right.'

'Very well! I'll get back to Rome as fast as I can.' He paused, and then changed the subject. 'Your car — how is it?'

'Beautiful. It's like new. I'll never be able to thank you enough for the repairs, Donato.' I bit my lip for having used his name as I saw Paul stiffen out of the corner of my eye. 'I'll go now,' I added. 'See you later.'

I hung up and turned immediately for the door. Paul moved forward, and I thought he was going to accost me, but he reached for the telephone. As he lifted the receiver he looked into my eyes.

'Don't leave, Gail. I'd like to have a chat with you. That was Donato you were talking to, wasn't it?'

'Yes, it was.' I kept walking to the door.

'He's in Florence right now, isn't he?'

'That's right.' I kept moving. My heart was thudding. 'He's coming back now.'

'Wait for me. I shan't be more than a few moments.'

'I'll be outside,' I said, and left the lobby.

But I had no intention of waiting for Paul. While I was in his sight I moved casually, but once I had crossed the terrace I ran to my car, my hand trembling as I fumbled with the key. I got in and switched on the ignition, revving the engine before slipping into gear. I watched the doorway of the hotel, and clenched my teeth when Paul suddenly appeared. When he saw me easing the car towards the exit he came running down the terrace steps, hurrying toward me, calling me urgently. He managed to get to the side of the car and bent to peer in at me. I depressed the button that locked the door.

'Gail, stop,' he called. 'I need to talk to you.'

I shook my head and drove out to the street. Paul grasped the door handle but I accelerated and he was flung aside. I glanced in the rear-view mirror and saw him stumbling. I pushed the car up to thirty. As I departed, my last sight of Paul showed him running back into the hotel courtyard.

A sigh escaped me as I drove on. That had been close! Paul had certainly wanted to be in my company, and Donato's warning had alerted me to my danger. I drove steadily, breathing heavily, determined not to get caught napping again. I would leave Rome for the evening and return later, in time to meet Donato at his home. By then perhaps Paul and Rinaldi would both be under arrest.

I kept glancing in the rear mirror, but Paul did not have a car and by the time he found transport I would be long gone. All I had to do was stay free until I could get to Donato. I drove south towards Frascati, twenty-four kilometres away in the Alban Hills; and although I was not in a mood for sight-seeing, I knew it was a most beautiful area. At least I could lose myself amid the many tourists.

My confidence began to return as I left Rome, and for the first time since leaving the hotel, my hands relaxed slightly on the wheel. I sighed heavily in relief and prayed for the next few hours to pass quickly, for then my nightmare would end. But I would have to be very careful when I returned to the city. When I had left Donato's home after meeting Lieutenant Madante, Paul and Rinaldi had been waiting outside in Rinaldi's car; and they could be waiting again when I returned, because Paul had overheard my telephone conversation with Donato, and then I had foolishly told him that Donato was returning later that evening.

Fresh worry welled up in my mind. How careful did one have to be when trying to deceive criminals? They seemed to cover every eventuality with ease, while at every turn I seemed to make the most elementary mistakes.

I drove into and around Frascati, then returned to Rome, lingering for a time on the outskirts, waiting for darkness to fall. My nervousness grew as the sun went down. I began to drive in the direction of Donato's home, aware that every passing car could be Rinaldi's, and that Paul would be looking for my Corsa. Perhaps that was why Rinaldi had been looking at my car when I arrived — he wanted to know exactly what it looked like.

I needed to find a street that I knew in order to get my bearings, and then drive along the route Donato had taken when he took me to his home to meet Lieutenant Madante. I had no difficulty finding my way, and when I drew near to the street where Donato's home was situated I parked in the shadows, switched off the lights, and sat gazing around, checking my surroundings. I was not going to make the mistake of driving straight into trouble; I had finished with acting like a complete fool at every turn. This time I was going to be just as smart as the criminals.

It would be safer to move in on foot, and I stayed in the shadows as I walked towards the driveway that led to Donato's villa, expecting at any moment to see Rinaldi's car. I walked slowly, like a fox emerging from its lair at first light with the smell of hounds on the breeze. I eased the strap of my shoulder bag and moved around the gatepost and into the garden of Donato's villa. In a few seconds I was lost in the dense blackness of deep shadow, and pressed my back against a tree, listening intently for any unnatural sounds. But there was only the wind sighing and rusting the foliage.

There were lit windows in the villa, and I walked slowly from tree to tree along the driveway, remaining under cover, my heart thumping as tension began to envelop me. Yet there was no cause for alarm; I was closer to safety now than I had ever been. But my eyes ached from the effort of trying to pierce the gloom, and when some small creature suddenly darted away with a skittering sound my heart lurched painfully and a throbbing hammered my temples. But I took a fresh grip on my nerves and continued.

Angling through the shrubbery proved to be a mistake, for almost immediately I was on rough ground and I lost my balance in the shadows, tripped over a protruding root, and fell sprawling full-length with sufficient force to drive the breath from my body. I struggled to my feet and leaned against a tree, lifting my right leg and rubbing my ankle. I had dropped my shoulder bag and bent to fumbled for it, uttering a silent prayer of thanks when my groping fingers came into contact with it, for my car keys were inside. I really had to pull myself together — imaginary shapes and figures were materialising out of the shadows, and I was ready to run screaming for the comparative safety of the street.

Before moving on, I heard the faint sound of shoe leather scraping on gravel somewhere very close. I froze, my breath catching in my throat. A moment later, safe in the impenetrable blackness, I saw the indistinct figure of a man moving slowly along the driveway towards the villa. I bent slightly, trying to get him silhouetted, and almost gasped aloud when I recognised the unmistakable outline of Paul as he passed before a bright window. What was he doing here? I had imagined he was out searching Rome for me. But he was going towards the house.

Hardly aware of what I was doing, I started back the way I had come, making for the gateway — but tripped again, falling over something hard and sharp that scraped skin from my left knee. The faint sound must have alerted Paul, for when I looked around he had paused and was looking in my direction. I knew he would come to investigate, and began to run, filled with a blind, unreasoning panic.

Twigs snapped under my trampling feet, and in the silence it must have sounded like a herd of stampeding elephants. I heard Paul's voice, demanding to know who was there, but I was only galvanised to greater effort. I burst out of the shrubbery and ran along the street like a person demented, trying to break the record for the quarter-mile. Although I was fast, I did not have much time to spare, for as I darted around the corner I looked back over my shoulder and saw Paul in hot pursuit.

Panting and gasping, I headed for the Corsa, fumbling in my shoulder bag for the car keys. They were ready in my hand as I reached the vehicle. I pressed the key, heard the car locks open, and hurled myself behind the wheel. My eyes were glued to the rear-view mirror as I started the engine, and when Paul came around the corner twenty yards from me I was already pulling away from the kerb, all doors and windows locked. I switched on the lights as the car changed up into second gear, and laughed in relief, for Paul had been beaten a second time that night. He halted as I zoomed away, and then turned without hesitation and returned the way he had come.

My body was clammy and beads of perspiration were dripping down my face. I had no idea where to go, and could only think that I would be safe on the move. I kept glancing in the mirror, forcing myself to remain within the speed limit. Thankfully, I saw no sign of pursuit, and turned several corners in quick succession, determined to lose Paul if he did have a car and was after me.

Suddenly a pair of headlights drew up behind me, and I clenched my teeth. Swinging around yet another corner, I braked immediately so that I was out of sight of the other driver, did a right-hand U-turn, and drove out of the street, turning back along the one I had just left. When I passed the car that had been behind me I turned my head and peered anxiously at it, trying to glimpse the driver. But it was too dark to see anything, and I heaved a ragged sigh as I drove on quickly. My heart sank when I glanced in the mirror and saw the other car doing a three-point turn. It could only be Paul, I thought, and he must have recognised my car. He did not have to look at me for identification.

The headlights in my rear-view mirror seemed to gain on me even though I was breaking the speed limit. I took a corner almost on two wheels and shuddered as my imagination went to work. I was a good driver, but not accustomed to driving under these conditions. I realised that speed alone would not beat Paul. He would drive as fast as road conditions would permit, and I felt that I could not match his skill. I would have to resort to other methods, and did so instantly, slowing and turning into a secondary road, hoping that I would not end up in a cul-de-sac. I cornered again, twisting through a back street, travelling slowly now, but making it difficult for any pursuer to guess at my general direction. In fact, I had no sense of direction. My only desire was to shake off pursuit, and I doubled back around a block of flats in a determined effort to lose my dogged tail.

Suddenly I recognised the road I was on and realised that I was again approaching the street where Donato lived. Almost immediately headlights showed up in the mirror. I could not afford to take any chances. I had to suspect that all other motorists on the road were Paul and act accordingly — but the car behind came up at such a tremendous speed, I was in no doubt as to the identity of the driver. The next instant it was alongside me; and when I glanced sideways, my eyes narrowing against the combined glare of two sets of headlights, I saw the pale oval of a man's face and recognised it as Paul.

He lifted a hand from the steering wheel and signalled for me to pull over. I gazed ahead and stepped on the pedal, surging away from him, and it was fortunate for both of us that this was a quiet area with little or no traffic about. But he came up alongside me again, and I was aware that he could put me off. He must be really desperate to stop me, and the knowledge made me all the more determined to get away.

I braked suddenly, for an intersection was coming up; and while Paul shot ahead I spun my wheel, still braking hard, and swung to the left, almost turning the car over. For several seconds I thought I had gone too far, but the Corsa kept on the road, although I was on the wrong side for some distance. Paul had driven straight on. I stopped immediately, turned the car, and drove back to the intersection. There was no sign of Paul's car, and I assumed that he had gone on to the next corner in preference to turning in the road. That had gained me some time and distance. But I had to get back to Donato's villa. He should be home by now, and was the only security I had. Even if he was not there I could telephone the police and ask for Lieutenant Madante. He would provide some protection!

But the headlights appeared in my mirror again and I clenched my teeth in frustration. I felt weak and shaken, my determination fading under the pressure being exerted on my nerves. I had been subjected to quite an ordeal in the past few days. The strain was beginning to tell, and I knew I could not go on much longer.

The pursuing car came up alongside me once more, but instead of waving me down, Paul cut across and pulled in front. I braked quickly, while he had to accelerate to get ahead. He overshot by quite a distance, and I started forward again as he began to turn in anticipation of me changing direction once more. Too late, he saw me bearing down on him, and I almost clipped him in passing; but he swung his wheel, hurling his car towards the kerb. I continued, peering in the mirror, and saw his front wheels mount the pavement. There was a terrific crash as he hit a lamp-post, and I laughed in triumph, for now he was really out of the picture. I gave no thought to the fact that he might be injured. I slowed down, driving more in keeping with the local driving regulations, and my last glimpse of Paul's car as I turned out of the street showed that it was well wrapped around the lamp-post, the top of which had crashed down on his bonnet.

But my attention should have been on the road ahead, and it was almost too late when I finally looked where I was going. There was a car parked without lights that I had not spotted, and I wrenched the wheel around to avoid it, gritting my teeth and freezing in the seat. I managed to avoid the car but lost control, skidding across the road before I realised that my foot was clamped down on the brake pedal. I released the brake to correct the skid, but spun around and hit the kerb with a jolt that flung me against the seat belt. If I had not been wearing it I would most certainly have gone through the windscreen, or at least smashed my head against some part of the car. But apart from being badly shaken and having stalled the engine, I was unhurt. I slumped in my seat for a few moments, fighting off an increasing weakness; but such was my fear of pursuit that I gathered myself for another effort and started the engine.

When I tried to move off I heard a grating sound from the right front wheel, and the car lurched unevenly. I had a flat tyre! Stopping, I alighted quickly and peered around nervously. When I looked at the right front wheel I saw that the tyre had burst and the wheel itself had buckled.

I could have cried, as much from disappointment at the wrecking of the fine repair job as from being stranded. But I was not far from Donato's villa, and there was nothing to prevent me walking the rest of the way, or running if I had to! I glanced around again, now wondering if Paul had been hurt when he hit the lamp-post. But I could not worry myself about him. He had put my life at risk with his desperate attempts to stop me.

There was a street lamp nearby, and as I turned to reach into the car for my shoulder bag I caught a gleam of light on a small white packet that lay on the road near my front wheel. I bent to pick it up and discovered that it was a sealed transparent plastic bag, and when I held it up to the light I could see that it contained a white powdery substance. Frowning, I looked down and saw two more similar packets on the road.

As I picked them up I glanced at the flat tyre and saw a gaping hole in its outer wall. Filled with impatience — for in the back of my mind was the fear that Paul was already pursuing me again — I bent over the wheel and examined the split in the tyre. My semi-dazed mind was even more bewildered when I discovered many other small white packets inside the tyre. An inner tube was showing through the split in the outer casing, its thin rubber hanging in tatters.

Thrusting some of the packets into

my shoulder bag, I straightened to check my surroundings. In the distance the lights of a car showed, and I tightened my grasp on my bag and hurried along the street to the nearest corner. I had to get to Donato's villa. It was the only sanctuary for me in the Eternal City of Rome, famous for its sanctuaries.

13

When I reached the driveway to Donato's villa, I did not bother sneaking through the shadows in the garden. I ran through the gateway and along the gravelled path, my shoes making plenty of noise. But speed was essential, and I was gasping for breath long before I saw the stark outline of the building. The lights were on in some of the ground-floor rooms, and I prayed that Donato had at last returned from Florence. Then I saw a car in front of the steps leading to the terrace and, drawing nearer, recognised it as the Fiat I had used. Donato had gone to Florence in it, so he was back!

I stumbled up the steps and rang the doorbell, turning to peer fearfully into the shadows edging the driveway. At any moment Paul's ominous figure could materialise. I rang the bell again, and the door was jerked open unexpectedly, jarring my nerves. Donato stood before me, and I uttered a little cry of relief and hurled myself forward into his arms.

'Gail, what is wrong?' He gazed past me. 'Where's your car?'

I began to explain in a rather incoherent tone, but Donato grasped my wrist and drew me into the villa. He closed and bolted the door.

'Come this way, quickly!' he said.

He led me into his study, which was through a door to the right. The light from its window had helped me find my way along the drive outside. A large briefcase was on the desk, and a sturdy safe was in a corner; its door was open and some papers were strewn on the floor in front of it.

'Just tell me where your car is,' said Donato. His expression was harsh, his dark eyes narrow. His forehead was furrowed, and for the first time since we had met I saw that he was quite emotional. I explained where I had left the car and told him about the damaged front wheel.

'Give me your keys. I'll go and change the wheel and then bring the car here. Paul Russell must not get his hands it.'

'He's tried hard enough to get his hands on it since you telephoned from Florence,' I said, opening my shoulder bag and taking out the car keys. One of the little plastic packets fell out of the bag, and I dropped the keys when I bent to pick it up. Donato snatched the packet from me, his fingers suddenly trembling.

'I found this and more on the road after my tyre burst,' I said urgently. 'And there are more inside the tyre itself.'

'But these are not packets of jewellery!' Donato frowned, his eyes filled with concern and wonder as he gazed at me.

'They look like packets of drugs,' I said. 'You'd better call Lieutenant Madante and report this to him. Paul could be at my car right now, and once he sees what's happened to that tyre he'll know his game is over.'

'Yes.' Donato's expression changed and he turned to the desk. Snatching up the telephone, he dialled a number, tapping his fingers impatiently as he waited for a reply. After a few moments he took the phone from his ear and looked at it before depressing the rest rapidly several times. 'This line is dead!' he cried.

'I told you Paul was in the driveway when I first arrived.' I went to the side of the desk, shaking my head worriedly. 'Perhaps he's cut the wires!'

'Give me your keys and I'll attend to the car. If I see him out there I'll tackle him. It could be that he was hurt in the crash. If he's not around, then I can call the lieutenant on another telephone.'

I gave him the keys and he hurried to the door, but paused to look back at me, shaking his head as I made to follow him. 'No. You stay here. It's too dangerous. I'll lock you in for safety's sake.'

I nodded and he departed, closing the door. I heard his footsteps crossing the hall, then silence. I turned to pace the room, fighting off reaction and praying that Donato would hurry. My knees were trembling. Then I noticed a newspaper was lying on the desk and reached for it, wanting something to occupy my mind. My imagination was running riot, thrusting up pictures of Donato being attacked by Paul, who had certainly changed his tactics since early evening. I looked at the front page of the paper, an evening edition; and despite the fact that I had been denying all knowledge of the Italian language since my arrival, I began to read the news.

A small photograph seemed to leap up off the page at me, and I gasped in horror when I realised that it was a picture of Alfredo Rinaldi. The caption beneath it informed me that Rinaldi, an Italian customs investigation officer, had been shot and wounded in a Florence back street that morning.

Rinaldi had been working to capture an international gang of drug smugglers. His condition was stable, and the arrest of the criminals was imminent.

I slumped back in the seat and gazed at the photo of the little man I had first seen snooping around my car at the hotel. But Donato had said that Rinaldi was a criminal! I closed my eyes as my mind teetered on the edge of insanity. My thoughts were in turmoil as I assimilated the facts. Rinaldi was *not* a criminal. So what about Paul? If Rinaldi was on the side of law and order, and apparently a good friend of Paul's, then who were the real criminals?

I covered my face with my hands and tried to close my mind to the knowledge that tried to force its inevitable way into the forefront of my thoughts. It was logical that Donato had been lying to me all along about the true situation. But he had been very close to Lieutenant Madante, and had insisted I should try to help the police. And Rinaldi had been shot in Florence, which was where

Donato had been for the last few days!

I was so badly shocked that I could not think straight. I again read the caption under the photograph. There was no other news about Rinaldi. I closed my eyes as I tried to pick out the truth from the web of deceit that had apparently been spun about me. Yet I also felt a sense of relief, for Paul could not possibly be a criminal, and I found that knowledge satisfying.

I began to reconsider Donato. He had obviously lied to me, but to what extent I could only guess. I thought he had been helping the police — Lieutenant Madante had been here in this very house. I glanced around the study, noting the obvious signs of hurried packing, and looked in the briefcase. There were business papers, but I had no time to read them. I looked at the papers on the floor in front of the safe and wondered why Donato was in such a hurry.

Moving to the door, I grasped the handle, but when I turned it the door did not open. I frowned as I exerted my strength to no avail. Donato had said he would lock me in for my own safety, but I imagined he meant to lock the front door, not the study. I went to the window, suddenly aware that no matter what happened I had to get out of this house. Drawing aside the heavy curtains, I saw with horror that bars were fixed to the outside of the window. I could not get out! Returning to the desk, I sat down and awaited Donato's return. What should my reaction be when he arrived? If he was the criminal, I should not confront him with the fact that I was aware of his deceit. I folded the newspaper and returned it to its former position on the desk, then arose and crossed the room to sit down on an easy chair by a shelf of books. It was my turn to act deceitfully. I needed the truth, and the only way to get it was by pretending to remain ignorant of what had really occurred.

Donato returned some time later, looking even more agitated than before.

I saw a dangerous glitter in his dark eyes that had not been there earlier. He was getting desperate. I wondered what I should say. But he spared me the problem of having to think of a course of action. He hurried to the briefcase on the desk, snapped it shut, and produced a small bunch of keys. His eyes flickered to me as he locked the case.

'I didn't try to change the wheel where you had left the car,' he said. 'I drove it on to some waste ground not far from here.'

'Did you see anything of Paul?'

'No.' He glanced around the room, went to the open safe, bent to scoop up the papers lying in front, then locked it.

'Did you call the police?' I asked.

'There was no time for that.' He came and faced me, looking into my eyes. 'We need to get away from here before Paul shows up. Once I've changed the wheel on your car, we'll go straight to the police.'

I didn't want to accompany Donato,

but a refusal might make him suspicious. I racked my brains for a plausible excuse. 'What are your plans?' I asked. I realised that I could not continue with apparent ignorance of the true situation. 'How did those white packets get into my tyre, Donato?'

'Rinaldi and Russell must have put them there after your car was returned to you.'

'I thought Rinaldi was a jewel thief. Does he also deal in drugs?'

'I don't know anything about that.'

'You're very nervous, Donato. Are you afraid of Rinaldi? Did Lieutenant Madante tell you that Rinaldi was a criminal?'

'Of course, and I recognised his picture in the rogues' gallery.'

'You're lying!' My voice was crisp and rang out startlingly clear. The suddenness of my accusation startled him.

'I don't understand!' He frowned.

'There's a picture of Rinaldi in that evening paper you brought from Florence. I'd better tell you now that I speak fluent Italian, and I read the paper while you were out.'

There was a shocked silence. I could feel the tension mounting. Donato was stiff, his breathing restrained. His face was pale, and there was a faint sheen of perspiration on his forehead. He sighed heavily. 'Are you working with Paul Russell?' he demanded hoarsely.

'No.' I shook my head. 'I seem to be the only one in this affair who really is what I claim to be. Paul Russell certainly isn't an insurance agent or a jewel thief. Is he connected with Europol, or a drugs squad, like Rinaldi? How did I get involved in all this — and why? I first saw Rinaldi when he was snooping around my car at the hotel the day I arrived in Rome. I never told you I could speak Italian, because I overheard the hotel receptionist on the telephone reporting my arrival and that I was alone with my car. What was so special about me and my car? You came on the scene when we had that accident, after which you took my car to a garage and had it repaired — with some added extras, like inner tubes in the tyres filled with packets of drugs.'

'You've been putting your mind to the situation, haven't you?' He shook his head as he spoke. 'But there is no time to explain. The police will be on their way here by now, and I must get away before they arrive.'

'So *you* are the criminal, not Paul. You told me Rinaldi was a jewel thief, but the evening paper said he was working for the law. I've been running away from Paul all evening, thinking he was a criminal, but now I realise he was trying to save me from you.'

'We've been using people like you for a long time to get our drugs into England,' he admitted with a ghost of a smile coming to his lips. 'But since you arrived there's been nothing but trouble. I didn't know Paul Russell earlier, and when I did find out about him it was too late. We deliberately damaged the cars of English holidaymakers, put drugs in their tyres, and removed them when they returned to England. It worked well until you showed up. When you followed Russell and Rinaldi the other night and saw them entering a building, I knew I was in trouble, because it was my father's garage. You inadvertently warned me just how close they were getting to me.'

'And of course Lieutenant Madante is not a policeman.'

'That's right. Pretty clever, don't you think? Madante is my right-hand man. But some of my gang became afraid, and that's why you had trouble with Monati at Ostia. The gang split right down the middle. Half of them wanted to suspend the drugs operation until the heat was off, and when I refused they thought they could scare you out.'

'So what happens now, Donato?' My mind was reeling with the revelations, but in the back of it relief was blossoming because of the knowledge that Paul was not a criminal.

Donato shrugged, motioning toward the door. 'We shall leave together, and if you don't give me any trouble then no harm will come to you. But I am desperate now. Help me get away and you will live to write your story about this business.'

'Do I have any choice?' I heard my voice as if a stranger were speaking, and wondered how I could talk so calmly.

He shook his head, put his right hand into his pocket and produced a small handgun. I looked into its muzzle and started to tremble. 'Please don't point that at me,' I said sharply. 'It scares me half to death. I'm not going to try and stop you escaping; I've had my fill of trying to help the police, even if they weren't real. Go ahead, get away, and good luck to you. Just leave me out of it. I only have one holiday a year, and this one has been ruined.'

He smiled, but his eyes were hard and filled with menace. 'I feel sorry for you,' he said. 'Your hotel receptionist was paid to supply me with information of any single Englishwoman with a car who booked in. You were trapped in our scheme before you actually arrived. But you became friendly with an undercover policeman and unwittingly led the law right to me. All this trouble is down to you, although you had no idea what was going on.'

'No,' I countered. 'You stuck your head right into their trap.'

'And you didn't know Russell is a Europol officer?'

'Do you think I would have spent all evening running away from him if I had?'

He shrugged. 'That's enough talking. I must leave now. Fortunately, I have an escape plan ready.'

'I'm not going with you!' I said firmly. 'I'm going to sit right here and wait for Paul to come for me. He was in your driveway earlier; obviously waiting for you to return from Florence. You won't escape, Donato.'

'Oh, I will. But I think I shall have to change my mind about you. I suspect you know too much. I'll have to silence you before I leave.'

'Don't be a fool!' I was chilled by his words.

'Perhaps it would be better to hold you until we get clear of Rome. Come with me if you want to live. Don't waste my time or attract attention to yourself. I shot Rinaldi in Florence, and if you become a burden to me then I'll shoot you as well.' He put the gun back into his pocket and patted the bulge it made. 'Don't forget I've got this, and remember that I can soon put this situation right. There are just two people I would have to kill to put the odds back in my favour.'

'I'm one, I assume,' I said shakily.

He nodded. 'And Paul Russell is the other.' He came close. 'We are going out to your car and I'll change the damaged wheel. I dare not use my own car, and I shall need the drugs in your tyres to make a fresh start somewhere else.'

He led me out of the villa and we walked down the densely shadowed driveway. I could not understand why there were no police around, and kept hoping that Paul would suddenly step out of the shadows to rescue me. Donato interrupted my thoughts as we reached the street. He directed me to walk to our left, and we went to where he had parked my Corsa. It was on a piece of open ground and barely discernible from the road. I saw that the car was tilted slightly because of the burst right front tyre.

'Get in the car and sit still while I change the wheel,' Donato said. 'Don't make me nervous by trying to escape. Just do as I say and everything will be fine.'

'Are you running out on your gang as well?' I asked as I opened the door of the car. 'Of course, I suppose none of them was arrested. Monati wasn't picked up for speeding, was he?'

'No. They've all gone underground temporarily. We've been prepared for something like this. Now stop talking. I'll change the wheel and we'll leave Rome. It's up to you how you come out of this. Give me any trouble and I'll send you and the car into a ravine. It will be an accidental death — a tyre burst and you swerved off the road.'

I hesitated for the barest moment, for it was obvious that death awaited me this night in one guise or another. Perhaps a bullet would be quicker and less painful! I did not feel afraid, because it all seemed so unreal — like a bad dream that could soon be forgotten. I got into the driver's seat and sat stiffly, aware that I might have a better chance of surviving if I waited until Donato was driving.

He slammed the door on me and went to the boot to get the spare wheel. I thought of jumping out of the car and making a run for it, but the thought of the gun in his pocket deterred me. I twisted in the seat to look through the rear side window at him. He was bringing the spare tyre alongside the car to the front wheel. Acting instinctively, my mind alive to all possibilities, I waited until he was level with my door before thrusting it open with all my strength. It hit him hard, then flew back at me, and I hastily pulled my legs back inside the car.

At that instant I became aware of another figure appearing within my field of vision, approaching from the shadows at the back of the car. It was Paul! Relief exploded inside me. I opened the door as Donato sprang to his feet. His right hand went quickly into his pocket, and it was not until then that he became aware of Paul's presence.

'He's got a gun, Paul!' I yelled, and my words acted as a signal to both men.

Donato pulled his gun out of his pocket as Paul launched himself forward in a low tackle. He made contact with Donato and they fell to the ground. I scrambled out of the car and ran forward, only to hear Paul calling to me.

'Switch on the car lights!' he yelled. 'I need to see what I'm doing.'

I turned breathlessly to the car and

obeyed, and when the darkness was dispelled I peered through the windscreen to see Donato lying face down on the ground. Paul was holding him in an arm lock.

'Sound the horn three times,' Paul said, his face averted from the glare of the lights.

I obeyed, and a few moments later several uniformed policemen appeared out of the shadows, closing in from different directions. Donato was quickly taken away. Then Paul came to the car where I was sitting, shocked, in the driver's seat.

'Thank you for your help,' he said lightly; but his handsome face was set harshly. 'You certainly gave me some problems earlier. I'd rather have you on my side.'

'It was your fault that I wasn't on your side from the beginning!' I retorted. 'I ought to be very angry with you for using me the way you did.'

'So di Barocci told you something of the situation.'

'I saw Rinaldi's photograph in the evening paper that Donato brought back from Florence. It told me nearly everything, and Donato filled in the gaps when I confronted him.'

Paul smiled. 'Rinaldi didn't want to use you at all, but you were the woman with the car di Barocci was interested in at the time we set up our trap, and we had no alternative but to drag you in.'

'That sounds like the hand of fate at work,' I observed acidly. 'What about the rest of Donato's gang?'

'You needn't concern yourself about them. While I was trying to save you from trouble this evening at di Barocci's villa, the Italian police — the *real* police, that is — were rounding up the gang.' His tone softened for a moment and he placed a gentle hand on my shoulder. 'You'll have to make a statement before you'll be free to enjoy what remains of your holiday. But before that, there is one thing I must do.'

'What's that?'

'Change your front wheel. I should have let Donato do that before I tackled him, but I knew he was armed and I didn't want to take any chances with your life.' He paused and pushed his face closer to mine, his keen blue eyes glistening in the glare of the headlights. 'Do you think you'll ever be able to forgive me for the way I used you? I took a lot of liberties.'

'Well, you've given me enough material to keep me writing for the next twelve months,' I laughed shakily. 'I'll forgive you if you'll meet me halfway and forgive me for believing Donato when he told me you were a criminal.'

He smiled. 'I'll forgive you freely if you tell me you cooled off towards me because you believed him.'

'That was the reason I put a hold on my feelings. You started the doubts in my mind, by the way.'

'How did I manage to do that?'

'When we first met you said you were an insurance agent, but I could tell it wasn't true.'

'All part of my cover story.' He paused and looked into my eyes. 'But in all the deceit and intrigue, I did tell you two things that were true.'

'Really?' I laughed lightly, my confusion and shock beginning to disappear. 'You'll have to explain, because I doubt I would recognise the truth from you.'

'I *do* live in London, and when we both get home I *shall* want to see you again. We were getting along really well before Donato turned up, don't you think?'

'That I do agree with. Let's start a clean page and go on from there.'

He put his arms around me, drew me close and cupped my chin tenderly. His lips were soft, arousing a passion I did not know I had in me. I realised instantly that the old magic of our first evening together was still alive and vibrant, despite what had happened since, and that was all I needed to know. And then, much to my dismay, he released me! I pouted, and he laughed.

'Come on, young lady,' he said,

chaffing me lovingly. 'I'd better get this wheel changed.'

I watched him set to work, hope blossoming in my heart. Suddenly, the future was looking wonderful . . .

Other titles in the
Linford Romance Library:

CHRISTMAS REVELATIONS

Jill Barry

Reluctant 1920s debutante Annabel prefers horses to suitors. When she tumbles into the path of Lawrence, Lord Lassiter, she's annoyed that this attractive man is the despised thirteenth guest joining her family for Christmas — for he has been involved in a recent scandal, and only he and his faithful valet, Norman Bassett, know the truth behind the gossip. Meanwhile, as Lawrence tries to charm Annabel, Norman has a surprise encounter with a figure from his past — one who has been keeping a secret from him for years . . .

WHERE THE HEART LIES

Sheila Spencer-Smith

Amy sets off to join her wildlife photographer boyfriend Mark on the Isles of Scilly, accompanied by her sister's dog Rufus, who she is dropping off with her sister's parents-in-law, Jim and Maria, at Penmarrow Caravan Site. But when she arrives, the park is deserted — except for the handsome Callum Savernack, who doesn't appear happy to have her there. When it emerges that Jim and Maria are temporarily unable to return to Penmarrow, Amy finds herself torn between her responsibilities to Mark, to Rufus — and to Callum . . .

THE SHADOW IN THE DARK

Susan Udy

Attempting to escape the scandal that has engulfed her, Daisy Lewis leaves home and heads for the Cornish town of Pencarrow, still as beautiful as she remembers from her childhood holidays. But news spreads like wildfire in the small, tightly knit community, and soon she must deal with a blackmailer who recognises her from her previous life. Even worse, she suspects it could be one of the two handsome men who are keen to romance her. Is there anyone Daisy can trust — and will her secret be exposed yet again?

ENCHANTMENT IN MOROCCO

Madeleine McDonald

Stranded in Morocco, Emily Ryan accepts a job offer from a stranger. Entranced by her new life in the sleepy coastal village of Taghar, she struggles to resist widower Rafi Hassan's charm — but also clashes with his autocratic ways and respect for tradition. As she attempts to persuade him to allow his teenage daughter Nour more freedom, Emily refuses to acknowledge her own errors of judgement. As the seasons turn and the olives ripen, Emily dares to dream of winning Rafi's heart — until danger threatens from an unexpected quarter . . .